A
Raven
Returns

Cover design by Books and Moods

Edited by Dayna Hart, Hart to Heart Edits

Proofread by Virginia Tesi Carey

Content Warning: contains adult themes and mentions of suicide and sexual abuse

DEAR READER,

I knew you'd be back. After all, it's time for you to meet Ash. Dark, broody, mysterious, and perhaps even danger-ous, he's the original raven. Finally, you'll learn why he created The Raven's Den, a gaming hell for rich men that's also a refuge for the women who need it most.

A h, The Raven's Den. Ash leaned contentedly over the balcony wall, looking down onto the busy gaming floor. His favorite sounds filtered up from below; glasses clinking, cards shuffling, men laughing, dice being thrown. All sounds that meant he was making money. He couldn't be seen where he dwelt in the darkness, but could survey everyone and everything in his domain, just the way he liked it.

It would be time to close soon, so leaning heavily on his raven topped cane, he made his way toward the stairs. He'd carried the cane since the day his father had died, a reminder of the monster he would become if he wasn't careful. It hadn't always had the raven on top, he'd added that around the time he opened this place. After having been shot in the leg a few weeks ago, it now served to support him physically, as well. The wound was bloody painful as he traversed the stairs. If he had been watching the gaming floor like he was supposed to rather than stewing over estate business, it never would have happened.

He pushed the heavy curtains open with his cane and ambled onto the gaming floor, breathing in the ever-present scent of liquor and tobacco.

Patrick strode across the floor toward him, his lips pressed in a disapproving line. "Giles and I are both here tonight, Ash, and perfectly capable of closing up. You didn't need to come down."

Ash waved Patrick away. "Stop coddling me," he growled. "Go up and see the ladies off for the night."

With a shake of his head, Patrick strode through the back curtain to do as he'd asked.

"Gentlemen!" Ash called out over the room of raucous men. "Say goodnight to the Lady Ravens!" He swept his cane through the air, gesturing for the ladies to make their nightly parade through the tables. Dressed in black, formfitting gowns that highlighted their curves and put their decolletage on full display, the masked ladies danced between the tables, waving their oversized, black feathered fans. The men whistled their appreciation as the ladies twirled and swayed their way to the back of the club where they disappeared, one by one, through the velvet curtains, each one blowing a kiss before she went. In his club, the ladies were there to be looked at, but never touched. The women were under his protection, and if any man so much as laid a finger on one of them, Ash would make sure the offending body part was broken before the bastard was thrown out.

"It's your last chance to win, gentlemen, so bet big. One final deal, spin, or roll. Good luck!" Cheers and clapping rose up as they all placed their wagers.

When the last of the cash and chips had been counted and locked up tight, Ash let out a long sigh. His leg ached and he needed a drink.

"Goodnight, you two," he said to Patrick and Giles. "Thank you for all your hard work."

They let themselves out through the backdoor. Ash's private quarters were attached to the club. A long hallway, with locked doors at both ends, crossed over the top of the alleyway behind the club and connected directly to Raven House. The Lady Ravens resided on the ground level of the building, and his rooms were on the upper floor. He filled a glass with brandy and sat at his piano, resting his cane carefully on top. The large, black instrument was the only piece of furniture in a wide open room. Its elegant curves were all Ash required.

Taking a long draw on the amber liquid, he tipped his head to each side, stretching the tense muscles of his neck. He placed the half empty glass on the coaster that lived on top of his piano and began to play. His signet ring winked in the lamplight as his fingers moved over the cool, ivory keys. Slowly, his eyes slid closed. Nothing eased his soul like his piano. It always had, even in his worst moments. He'd never been one to play works written by the greats. Instead, he allowed his heart to lead the way, unleashing the notes from within him. Sometimes grandiose, sometimes upbeat, sometimes passionate. Tonight... melancholy, with a little uncertainty and agitation thrown in for good measure. And fear, if he was honest.

He didn't want to face what he knew was coming, his inevitable return to his estate, Woodburn Hall, and the terrors from his past which would undoubtedly haunt him upon his arrival. He hadn't been back since his father's funeral seventeen years ago. Once his monster of a sire was dead, he'd fled, planning to never look back. But now someone was causing trouble. At the very least, his estate manager was stealing from him. He needed to put a stop to whatever was happening, and unfortunately that meant returning to his estate, whether he wanted to or not.

He slammed his hands down on the keys in an explosion of dissonant notes. He blew out a breath to calm himself. It wasn't the piano's fault. Carefully, he lowered the wood cover and reached for his glass, draining the remaining liquid down his throat.

The door to his quarters opened and his valet entered with a raised brow. He'd probably heard Ash's outburst from the stairwell.

"Is everything ready for us to leave in the morning, Fogg?"

He nodded solemnly. "Are you sure you don't want Patrick or Michael to go with you?"

Ash shook his head. "I need them here to take care of the club and everything else. It's not as if there will be any real danger. I just need to see to my estate for a bit."

"It's not the physical danger I'm worried about, Ash. You'll have me with you, after all."

"I don't really know who or what I will become in that place, especially with the plan we've decided on, and if they are worried about me, they'll intervene and get in the way. Have you forgotten they forced ether over my face and injected me with morphine after I was shot?"

"Yes, well, I would have helped them, if I had been here. You were being a stubborn fool."

"Perhaps I was, and I may be now, as well. But they're not coming. If things change and I need them, I can send a telegram and I have no doubt they'll be on the very next train."

He rubbed his aching leg before pushing himself to his feet. He needed sleep. Unfortunately, this was not one of those things that would be better in the morning.

———

Gwen stared across the room into her husband's angry eyes. She'd only meant to slip into his study long enough to grab some stationery, but then she'd seen the letters.

Letters to her husband, from a woman who seemed to think she was his wife.

"What are you doing in my study, Gwendolyn?" He folded his arms sternly across his chest and leaned against the doorway, blocking her only escape.

"I'm sorry, Greg. I was just looking for some—"

With the merest raise of an eyebrow he ordered her silence. Gwen swallowed as fear churned in her stomach.

"You know you're not allowed in my study, unless you've been invited." His calm tone didn't fool her. She was going to pay dearly for her curiosity. How had this happened? He had been so sweet to her right up until the day of their wedding, but then he'd suddenly changed, as if he'd been flipped to the opposite side of a coin. Lately, he'd grown to resent her. He seemed to revel in her pain and humiliation a little more each day.

With a nod toward the desk, he gave his instructions, but she didn't want to comply. Tears pricked the corners of her eyes. He lifted the leather strap from where it hung on the side of his bookshelves.

She walked slowly around to the opposite side of the desk, her heart galloping inside her chest and her throat aching as she tried to hold back her tears. Her body trembled as she laid herself across the hard wooden surface.

Greg slowly approached, and her fear and anger clashed creating an explosion inside of her. As he bent to lift her skirts, her hand shot out and grabbed the candlestick beside her. She spun around, swinging wildly until it connected with a sickening thud. Greg crumpled to the floor.

Dropping the candlestick, she clapped both hands over her mouth. What had she done? Was he dead? Oh lord, she was going to hang. She instantly hated herself for the thought. What kind of horrible person would think that before anything else? A groan issued from his mouth, and for a moment, she praised God. But if he was alive, that meant he could beat her, and he surely would now. She grabbed the letters from the desk and stuffed them into her waistband. After one last glance down at Greg, she sprinted from the room. More groans floated out behind her, pushing her onward.

Gwen ran, as fast as her feet would carry her, to the stables. Thank heavens the groom hadn't yet removed the saddle from Greg's horse. She tugged the reins out of the man's hands and launched herself onto the horse.

She urged the beast forward, but it was agitated by her abrupt appearance and stamped about briefly before obeying her. It had cost her precious seconds and Greg arrived just as she finally exited the stables. He grabbed onto her boot, nearly pulling her off of the horse. With a screech and a desperate tug, her foot came free of the boot and with the other one, she kicked the animal into motion.

"Fifty strokes await you when you return," he called out as she galloped away from him.

"I'm not coming back!" she shouted over her shoulder.

He simply shook his head. "Where will you go?"

It was true. She had nowhere else to go, but the mere threat of fifty strokes set her backside ablaze. If she returned, she would indeed feel the sting of the leather strap. She leaned low over the horse's neck and urged it faster and faster away from the house.

CHAPTER
TWO

Woodburn Hall loomed over Ash as he stood outside the front door. It was a monstrosity of a house. He breathed in deeply, steeling himself for what had to be done. Everyone here needed to believe him to be the same tyrant as his father if he wanted his plan to work. Giving a last look at Fogg, he nodded and wrenched open the heavy door.

Ash strode into the large entry hall. A footman gasped at his sudden intrusion, nearly dropping the silver candelabra he was carrying. Ash hadn't given any warning that he was coming.

After a few seconds, the footman sank into a deep bow, eventually recognizing who Ash must be. "My lord."

Ash closed his eyes, centering himself. No one addressed him by his title and hearing it after all this time made his skin crawl. In Ash's mind, his father was still Lord Ashdown, despite the fact he'd been dead seventeen years. He let out a long sigh. He needed to play the role to perfection in order to set expectations for his visit. He straightened himself to his full height, drawing his shoulders back.

"Where is Moulton?" he barked.

The butler appeared from an adjoining hallway. Tall, perfectly starched, and not a single dark hair out of place, just as Ash remembered, except for the grey creeping in at his temples.

"Sam, go to the—" Moulton stopped mid-sentence, his eyes growing wide as they landed on Ash. "My lord!" He hurried over, holding out a hand for Ash's hat and coat, but Ash didn't remove them.

"Moulton, this is my man, Fogg. He is to have unfettered access to every room in Woodburn Hall."

"Y... yes, my lord." Moulton tried to hide his confusion, but it showed on his round face nonetheless.

"And I mean, unfettered access, Moulton. If he chooses to go through the nightstand of a housemaid, he is to be left to his business. If he requires keys or access to anything, including in my private chambers or study, you will provide it without question. Any orders he may give are to be followed as if they were my own. Do I make myself clear?"

The butler straightened his spine and nodded. "Yes, my lord." He hadn't had anyone to answer to in a very long time. Ash desperately wanted to put the older man at ease and assure him he wasn't the overlord his father had been, but he needed him to believe otherwise for the time being.

"Right," Ash said, tapping his cane, the sound muffled by the thick carpet. He was glad to see everything at least appeared to be kept up as it should, even in his absence. He turned to Fogg. "I'm off before I lose all light."

"Yes, my lord." Ash cringed inwardly. It was even worse to hear those words from Fogg's mouth. He only ever addressed him as Ash or boss, but he, too, needed to play a role here. "It looks like it may rain," he warned.

"Not to worry, Fogg. I may have been away for a while, but I grew up here. I know this estate like the back of my hand. I'll find shelter if need be."

Ash managed to ride to the outer edge of his property before the clouds really began to thicken. This time of year, darkness came early anyway, but he had hoped for a couple of hours to check for any signs of recent repairs, or things just not as they should be. So far, there was nothing obvious, but he'd seen only a fraction of the sprawling property, so he kept going, even as an icy raindrop landed on his cheek.

He guided his horse into the trees, but when the sky opened up, even they provided almost no protection from the pounding rain. Fortunately, there was a small hunting cabin nearby. He'd take shelter there until it eased up a bit.

The disused, wooden structure still stood, if a little worse for wear. The cold made Ash's leg ache as he climbed down from the saddle. The attached stable, if you could call it that, was every bit as run down as the cabin, and devoid of anything for his horse. At least it offered shelter from the elements, and they wouldn't be here long.

Ash pulled his gloves off as he made his way around to the front of the cabin. He opened the door and stumbled backwards as a horse bolted through, nearly trampling him, and knocking his hat right off his head. "What the blazes?" His heart pounded in rhythm with the horse's hooves as it galloped away through the trees.

Before he could turn back to see what else might be inside the cabin, something hard landed against his shoulder, sending pain shooting down his arm.

"Ouch! What in the—" He grabbed hold of the fire poker, which was being wielded by a small, blonde, half-naked woman. What in God's name was happening?

She gasped as he yanked the weapon from her hands and curled herself down at his feet, her arms covering her head for protection. "I'm sorry." Her voice was tight with panic. "I'm sorry. Please don't hurt me."

She thought he was going to hit her. "Christ," he muttered, throwing the damned poker back into the cabin. He crouched beside her, trying to calm himself before speaking again. "I'm not going to hurt you."

Slowly, she lowered her arms and peeked up at him.

He recognized that face. He'd never seen it laced with such fear, but he would know this woman anywhere.

"Gwen?"

Relief washed over her. "Ash?" A smile grew on her lips, and she threw herself at him, sending him tumbling onto his back. As she landed on top of him, his hands came to rest on her very bare, very lush backside. They squeezed the soft, cold flesh without him even giving them permission to do so, and arousal instantly stirred in his loins. She gave a soft moan, shoving him back into reality. Christ, what was he doing?

He tore his hands away from her body, holding them up by his head. "I'm so sorry, Gwen."

"I'm not." Thank God the fear was gone from her eyes, but the daring sparkle that had replaced it brought about its own terror.

"No. No, no, no. Get up. Off." He seemed to have lost the ability to speak more than a single word at a time.

Pulling himself together, he reached for his cane and got to his feet, every inch of him soaked through. "Get back inside before you catch your death," he ordered.

Try as he might, he couldn't wrench his eyes away from her bottom as she turned and walked into the cabin. Her wet chemise clung to every curve. The water had also made the fabric mostly transparent, and lines striped the skin of her bottom. Having had similar marks across most of his body when he was young, he knew instantly what had caused them.

"Who hurt you?" His voice shook with barely contained fury. He would kill whoever had done it.

She whipped around, her eyes wide once more. She took a step back from him.

"I don't know what you're talking about." Her voice was high and breathy. Her eyes darted about the cabin.

"I saw the marks, Gwen."

"It's nothing, Ash." She shook her head, her gaze fixed on the floor.

"Who was it?"

"Please, Ash, it's nothing."

"Is he here with you?"

She shook her head, but panic filled her eyes when they looked up at him. "I hope not." Tears spilled down her cheeks, each one singeing his heart. In two strides, he had his arms wrapped around her. Her body trembled, probably from a combination of cold and fear. At least the cold he might be able to help with. She didn't fight him as he steered her to a chair and encouraged her to sit. Fetching some towels, he shook the dust out of them as best he could before handing them to her.

"Take that wet clothing off and I'll get a fire going."

"No!" She shot out of the chair. "You can't start a fire. He might find me."

Ash placed his hands on her shoulders. "You're safe now, Gwen. I promise you, whoever this person is, they won't make it through that door alive now that I'm here. All you need to worry about is getting warm and dry." He pointed back to the chair where she'd left the towel. With a hesitant nod, she returned and picked it up. Ash turned his back and peeled off his wet coat before setting to work on the fire. After seeing the fear on Gwen's face, he'd happily pummel the man to death.

"Are you covered?" Ash asked over his shoulder.

"Yes," she said quietly.

He dragged a chair in front of the fire. "Good. Have a seat."

She did as she was told and Ash hung their clothes near the fire to dry. Her dress and corset were easy enough to find, but something was missing. "I'm sorry to be indelicate, Gwen, but where are your drawers?"

Her cheeks immediately flushed. "I don't— He doesn't—" She paused before settling for, "There aren't any."

A blaze of fury nearly choked him. She didn't have to finish the statement for him to understand. Somehow, there was a monster in her life, controlling her, and he didn't allow her to wear them because they would restrict quick access if he chose to dole out punishment. He pressed his shaking fingers over his lips, his teeth in danger of shattering from his tightly clenched jaw. What had happened to her since she'd left Raven House? It couldn't have been more than eighteen months ago now.

"Is it your employer, Gwen? Did I send you into the care of someone who abuses you?"

Her head whipped around. "No." Her brow furrowed

and she shivered. Drawing one side of her bottom lip between her teeth, she looked into his eyes. "It's my husband." She ducked her head. "Or at least, I think he's my husband."

Before Ash could even formulate his next question in this mess, she looked up at him again. "What are you doing here, Ash?"

He folded his arms across his chest and leaned against the mantle. "This is my cabin."

"I don't understand."

Ash hated crossing these two parts of his life. "I expect you don't." He crossed one foot over the other, giving his sore leg a break, and let out a long sigh. "This is my estate, Gwen."

"All of it?" She dragged the words out slowly, still not fully understanding.

"Yes." He nodded, dreading the next words out of his mouth. Speaking them somehow made him feel pompous and dissolute at the same time. "I'm the Earl of Ashdown."

Gwen's mouth slowly fell open. She eventually closed it and blinked three times before taking a breath. "Since when?"

Ash chuckled. He hadn't been sure what she was going to ask next, but that wasn't it. "Since my father died. Seventeen years ago."

"But that means..." Her lips turned up in a slow

smile. "That means, when I was working as a Lady Raven, I was working for an earl."

A laugh startled from Ash. "Yes, I suppose you were."

"With all due respect, you're not really what I would have imagined an earl to be."

"I'm glad to hear it."

She continued to stare at him, seemingly in awe. That was why he didn't like telling people. Nothing had changed. He was still the same person he'd always been to her, and yet, in her mind, he was different.

"Now, Gwen, I know you don't want to talk about it, but I need to know how you came to be here, which means, you're going to have to start at the beginning. How did you end up with this husband of yours?" The words left a bad taste in his mouth. "Last I knew, you were working as a kitchen assistant in a household a very long way from here."

That seemed to break something loose so she was able to talk about it. "I was, but after a few months, I met Greg. He approached me at the market while I was picking up an order of lamb. After that, I seemed to bump into him every time I went to the market. He was all smiles and kindness, always complimenting me and bringing me small gifts. It wasn't long before I was smitten." Her shoulders fell slightly, and exhaustion seemed to settle over her. "So when he proposed marriage, I didn't even hesitate to say yes. He didn't want a big, proper wedding, so we eloped to Gretna Green."

She went quiet for a long moment, staring down at the hands in her lap. "That night, everything changed." She didn't look up, but Ash could see the quivering of her chin. God, what had he done to her? Sobs suddenly broke over her and she covered her face with her hands.

"Gwen." He knelt down and wrapped his arms around her shoulders. His heart broke for her. He would hunt the bastard down and kill him, slowly and painfully, just as soon as she was somewhere safe.

"I'm sorry," she said, trying to wipe the tears away.

"Shhhh. You never have to apologize to me, Gwen."

Slowly, she began to calm. She rested her head on his shoulder and he breathed in her sweet scent. If only he could stay like that forever. That was the thought that made him pull away from her. Keeping her safe meant he needed to adhere to his rules.

"That doesn't explain why you're here tonight, Gwen. What happened to send you out into this storm, with no coat and only one boot?"

She shrugged. "Greg was going to punish me. I panicked. I knocked him unconscious with a candlestick and stole his horse."

That was the Gwen he knew. She'd always been head-strong and courageous. "Are you sure he's still alive?"

"Yes." She nodded. "That's why I'm missing a boot. He tried to pull me off the horse."

Ice crept up Ash's spine at the thought of what would have happened to her if he had succeeded.

"Then I just rode, pushing the horse as fast as it would go. The rain started, and I needed shelter." She looked up at him. "And here I am."

"And here you are," Ash repeated, sadness filling his heart. "You're safe now, Gwen. I promise you." But then he remembered something else. "You said earlier that you *think* he's your husband. What did you mean by that?"

"I found some letters in his study." She pointed to a pile of papers on a small table near the bed. "That's why I was in trouble, actually."

Ash flattened the pages and read. It was clear this man was not legally married to Gwen. These letters were from his wife asking if he had managed to get 'the maid' with child yet. As horrific as it was, it would seem the wife was barren and had sent her husband to create a child with someone else to claim as their own. Nausea roiled in Ash's stomach. That someone was Gwen. In addition to beating her, how many times had he forced himself on her in his crusade to get her pregnant?

"Christ," he muttered, spearing his fingers into his damp hair.

"He's not— We're not—?"

Ash shook his head to confirm what she was asking. Neither of them had the strength to say it aloud.

"What am I going to do? I ran away from a good position. I believed he loved me. And now I have no husband, no employment, and nowhere to go." A hiss of cynical laughter made its way between her lips. "I don't even have a full pair of boots or drawers."

He placed a hand on her shoulder. "You're going to be alright, Gwen. You'll come with me. I'll make sure you're safe and have everything you need."

She scrunched her brow. "But why? Why would you do all of that for me? Again?"

Ash shrugged. "Because I can." Because it wasn't possible for him not to. He would never leave her without knowing she was safe and cared for. "When I finish my business here, I'll be returning to Raven House, and you will come with me."

"We can see how well I did with that the first time around." She huffed another laugh. "How many times are you going to save me, Ash?"

He lifted her chin gently. "As many times as it takes."

She stood then and pressed her lips to his, reaching one hand down and rubbing her fingers over his manhood, which greedily sprang to life inside his damp trousers. With the other hand, she pulled open the towel she was wrapped in and let it fall to the floor. Desire like he'd never known crashed over him, and it terrified him.

Gently, he placed his hands on her shoulders, holding her still while he stepped back from her. She was only behaving this way because she was in a state of shock.

"No, Gwen. I can't do this."

"Am I not to your liking?"

Before he could stop it, his gaze roved over her body

from head to toe and back up to her face. "You are the most beautiful creature I've ever laid eyes upon."

"Then why won't you let me give myself to you? My body is the only thing I have to give in return for your kindness. And I know you want it." She reached for his trousers again, but he quickly stepped back out of reach.

He shrugged one shoulder. "You know why, Gwen. It's against my rules." He would never again allow himself to take advantage of a woman because of his position.

She chuckled cynically. "It's not as if I'll be ruined."

It was time to head her off before his resolve gave out completely. "Before you cover yourself again, turn around so I can see the marks and make sure they don't need any kind of medical attention."

That did knock her off course. "It's nothing, Ash."

"Then allow me to look. I'll do nothing untoward."

She rolled her eyes. "Obviously."

"Please?"

With a huff, she spun around and bent over, placing her hands on the chair. The anger sparked by the marks was the only thing that allowed him to keep his wits about him with her in that position. There were a couple that were red, and swollen, and can't have been more than a day or two old. And so many others in various stages of healing. How many times had she endured his beatings?

He touched a fingertip to the edge of one and she

sucked in a breath. God how he wished he could take the pain from her and suffer with it himself, instead.

"I'm so sorry, Gwen. A few of these look quite painful, but I don't think there's much to be done to help, aside from time."

She stood, wrapped herself in the towel once more, and sat down.

"How often did he beat you?"

She shrugged. "Not very often in the beginning, but it became more frequent as the months passed. I think he was angry that I hadn't yet conceived a child. Those efforts became more frequent too, as they always immediately followed the punishment, but I was never successful." His heart broke for her as he once again vowed to hunt the man down and end him.

"Why don't you come and lie on the bed? That way you can at least avoid sitting on the wounds."

She shrugged again, her agitation growing. "Perhaps I deserve the pain."

Ash closed his eyes. How often had he said those same words?

Rather than arguing, he simply pulled back the blanket. "Come. Climb in."

With a huff, she eventually acquiesced. She dropped the towel before lying on her side in the bed. He pulled the cover over her shoulder and tucked her in.

"Will you hold me, Ash? I promise I won't try to seduce you again."

Ash chuckled. "Just this once." How could he possibly say no to those sad eyes? She looked so defeated. He climbed over her and squeezed his large frame between her and the wall, wrapping his arm around her and pulling her tightly against him. Even through the blanket, he could feel her curves. This was going to be one of the longest nights of his life.

"Get some sleep, Gwen." To his surprise, she did. He didn't know what he was going to do with her, but he would track down the bastard who had hurt her, and skin him alive for what he'd done.

THREE

Gwen was a little disappointed when she woke. She didn't even want to open her eyes. She'd been having a wonderful dream. Ash, 'Lord Ashdown', had saved her, once again, like a knight in shining armor. Even in her sleep-addled brain she laughed at the ridiculousness of it all. But when she did eventually allow her eyes to open, he was there, standing in the middle of the room. His clothes were a rumpled mess and he was tying an equally rumpled tie around his neck. It didn't detract from the glorious shape of his body, though. The black fabric still hugged his tight backside and broad shoulders. She'd always been drawn to him in a way she couldn't really explain.

Shame filled her belly as she remembered her behavior from the night before, throwing herself at him like some trollop. She might as well be. She'd been offering her body up as payment, after all.

He was nothing short of beautiful. Like an angel. A dark angel. She'd never seen him dressed in anything but black from head to toe. His dark hair was a bit unruly this morning and the shadow of a beard covered his face. So unlike him. Ordinarily, there was not a wrinkle to be found in his clothing, and not a hair out of place. But even as he was, confidence, power, and grace radiated from every inch of him. His station was so obvious. How had she never realized he was of the nobility?

"What's so funny?" he asked without even looking her way.

"I thought I must have dreamt you up. Lord Ashdown, saving me from utter peril, once more."

He finished with his tie and turned to face her. "Surely, if your mind had made it all up, you'd have at least been in a soft bed and warm."

"Perhaps you're right." But she had been warm, and safe, in his arms. She yawned and stretched. As she sat up, she pulled the blanket with her to cover herself. Her cheeks warmed remembering how she'd paraded around the cabin naked, as if it were a perfectly normal thing to do in front of a man.

"I'm sorry, Ash. Last night was— let's just say I was not on my best behavior, and I apologize for any embarrassment or uneasiness I may have caused you."

He crossed the room and crouched before her, raising

her chin gently to look into her eyes. "You don't need to apologize to me, Gwen. Last night was not a typical night for you. We'll just forget the whole thing happened, and move forward."

He might forget, but she would always remember. Even now, she could feel the heat of his strong hands gripping her backside as she lay on top of him in the rain. She gave him a small nod and a meek smile. "I don't know what I did to deserve you, Ash."

A self deprecating smile grew on his lips, then. "It's funny how those same words can have such a different connotation in my own head." He stood and moved away from her, a slight unevenness in his stride.

"What happened to your leg?"

He waved a hand as if it was nothing. "Somebody shot me."

Gwen gasped, but Ash simply shrugged. "It's nothing serious, but the thing doesn't seem to want to stop hurting. A bloody nuisance, honestly."

He donned his wrinkled coat and picked up his cane. "I'm going to step out and give you some privacy to dress. I need to get back before they send out a search party." He opened the door but then stopped and turned back. "Oh, and as much as I hate to ask this of you, I'm going to need you to address me by my title while we're here. I can't have my staff questioning my authority in any way at the moment."

And just like that he was gone. No further explanation. She wasn't even entirely sure what that meant. She dressed herself as best she could in her soiled, wrinkled clothes. What was she supposed to do with one boot? Should she just leave it behind? Or carry it with her?

That decision was made for her. When she walked out the door, Ash grabbed the boot and threw it back inside. "We'll get you a new pair."

She sighed and pressed her lips into a thin line. "I don't have any money, Ash."

"That's not something you need to worry about. I'm sure I can scrape together enough for a pair of boots." He winked, trying to make light of it.

"I don't want to be a charity case, Ash."

He placed his hands gently on her shoulders. "The money doesn't matter to me. Your welfare and comfort do. So, from this moment forward, you just start addressing me as my lord, instead of Ash, and I'll buy you all the boots you need. Can you do that?"

She couldn't help but smile. "Yes, my lord."

"Thank you."

An hour later, Gwen preceded Ash through the front door of his massive home. She had never seen such opulence. The thick carpet was soft beneath her bare feet. Huge portraits, presumably of his ancestors, adorned the walls and marble busts sat atop decorative column-like plinths between them. She wasn't sure how to feel about such extravagance. It was so opposed to what she knew about Ash.

"Fetch Mrs. Archer," Ash ordered as he handed his hat and coat to a waiting footman.

"Yes, my lord." The man scurried to do his bidding.

A short, stout woman of middling years rushed into the hall a few minutes later, a large chatelain rattling against her dark skirts.

"My lord, how may I be of service?"

"Mrs. Lawrence and I are both in need of baths. She will also need a change of clothes and a room to stay in."

Apparently Gwen was now Mrs. Lawrence. She tried not to allow her surprise at the announcement to show on her face.

"Yes, my lord. Where would you like me to put her?"

"In the room next to mine."

Gwen again tamped down her desire to whip her head toward Ash. For a brief second, the housekeeper's brow furrowed.

"Is that a problem, Mrs. Archer?"

"No, my lord. Of course not."

"Then see that it's done," he demanded. "And I will not tolerate any disrespect or gossip. Is that clear?"

"Yes, my lord." She dipped a curtsey and Ash strode away without a backward glance. Gwen had never seen him treat anyone so harshly before, and it shook her.

"This way, Mrs. Lawrence." It took a moment for Gwen to realize the housekeeper was addressing her. She swallowed down her apprehension and followed in her wake. The housekeeper rattled off orders to a half dozen other servants before they eventually arrived at a large bedchamber. When they entered, maids were still scurrying about, uncovering the furniture and dusting.

The housekeeper turned to face her. "Apologies, Mrs. Lawrence. We weren't prepared for a guest."

Gwen gave her a kind smile. "It's quite understandable, Mrs. Archer. I appreciate you making me welcome."

She followed the woman into the dressing room where a bath was already being filled. Mrs. Archer looked her up and down. "What kind of clothing do you require, Mrs. Lawrence?"

"Just anything clean will do. Don't make a fuss on my account."

Sinking down into the hot water a short time later was absolute bliss. The tub was so large she could even stretch out. Surely, she would be spoiled for all other baths after this. Mary, the maid, who'd been assigned to help her, had even drizzled some rose scented oil into the water. She'd never had a maid wait on her before, and it felt a bit awkward, but this seemed important to Ash, so she needed to play her part.

"How do you like working for Lord Ashdown?"

She shrugged as she scrubbed Gwen's hair. "I've never actually met him. In fact, most of us haven't."

That seemed strange. "Has he been gone so long?"

The girl nodded. "From what I understand, he never stayed a single night here after the late Lord Ashdown's funeral."

So why was he here now?

————

Fogg's raised brow was the only sign that he even noticed Ash's rumpled state as he strode into his father's dressing room. He gritted his teeth, holding back the memories. So many horrors had happened within these walls. Once the bath was ready, Fogg ushered the other servants out before helping Ash to undress. He was even more aware of Ash's wishes sometimes than he was himself. Fogg knew he wouldn't want the other servants to see his scars.

"Rough night?" Fogg asked as Ash sank down into the steamy water. He handed Ash a cloth and a bar of soap.

"You have no idea." He set to the task of removing the layers of dirt, wishing he could also scrub away the memories of this awful place. How could a house so large feel as if it were closing in around him?

"I heard you returned with a woman."

"How the hell did you hear that? I've only been back five minutes."

"It's only to your detriment to underestimate the speed at which gossip can travel through a household."

"Apparently."

"Who is she? Because I know she isn't your mistress."

"It's Gwen."

Fogg's brow furrowed deeply. "Gwen? Lady Raven Gwen? *Your* Gwen?"

"She's not *my* Gwen," Ash spat.

Fogg held up his hands. "Apologies, boss, I didn't mean to insinuate anything."

Ash glared at Fogg. The man was far too perceptive for his own good. Of course he would have known Gwen was something special. She always had been, from the moment she'd tried to pick his pocket. His heart ached at the memory. It felt so long ago now.

"Yes, that Gwen."

Fogg's eyes narrowed. "What is she doing here?"

Ash stepped out of the tub and began drying off. Even the hot bathwater couldn't chase away the icy cold inside these walls. Or perhaps these walls just made it emanate from within him. Ash shrugged. "I don't know exactly. I found her in a hunting cabin, sheltering from the rain."

"I don't like a coincidence," Fogg said quietly, his brows plunged into a deep vee.

"Neither do I. I will need your help with something concerning her, as well, but for now, tell me what you were able to discover while I was discommoded."

"Well, your estate manager has certainly made himself at home in your study, which was helpful of him. He obviously thought you'd never return. Full ledgers of his activities, just sitting in unlocked drawers. I still don't fully understand all the details. There's definitely some theft, as you suspected, but there also seems to be some kind of blackmail scheme?"

"Blackmail? Who is he blackmailing? And for what?"

"That's what I don't know, I'm afraid."

"The tenants?"

"I don't think it can be. The sums are far too great. I'll need to reach out to some of my contacts and see what they can dig up. But there's something else."

Fogg's pause was not a good sign. "What?"

"I believe he is somehow connected to the robbery."

"This robbery?" Ash pointed to the healing scar above his knee.

Fogg nodded grimly. "We knew it wasn't random, but I didn't think a connection would show up here. It's just too much of a coincidence to find information about your club in a desk drawer in this house, for your manager to not be involved in some way."

Ash sighed loudly and scrubbed his hands against his face. "Well, since you'll be reaching out to your network, have a look through the letters you pulled out of my coat pocket."

Fogg opened the pages and read through them, his eyes growing wider with each passing line.

"Gwen?"

Ash nodded. "I need to know everything there is to know about that man so I can destroy him." He might have been too young to protect his mother and brother, but he was no longer that scared boy. Now, he would do whatever was necessary to protect the people around him. That man would die for what he did to Gwen.

Fogg gave a single nod and slipped the pages into his own breast pocket. He obviously hadn't missed the barely bridled anger in Ash's voice.

"If I leave, who's going to see to you?" Fogg asked. "I'm still not sure who you can trust here, and you can't very well be the despotic Lord Ashdown without a valet."

"I have someone in mind. Benson was my father's valet until he one day refused to continue administering my beatings and my father threw him out."

Even Fogg blanched slightly at the words.

Ash nodded. "I've kept loose tabs on him over the years. He lives about an hour's ride from here. I believe I can probably convince him to come and work for me while I'm here. Perhaps it will give me a chance to make amends for some of the damage my father caused him."

"You know," Fogg said quietly, "it isn't actually your job to make amends for your father's wrongdoings."

"And it isn't your job to coddle me," Ash snapped.

"Yes, my lord." Fogg bowed deeply, all the while raising a challenging brow. Ash sighed and snatched his tie out of the man's hand.

"Point taken," Ash grumbled. Being back here was definitely making him grumpy, but Fogg recognized the words for the apology they were.

"What of Gwen? What do you mean to do with her while you're here?"

"I don't bloody well know." He scrubbed his hands over his face, once more. "She wasn't supposed to be a part of this whole goddamn mess."

"Might I make a suggestion?" Fogg straightened Ash's tie and reached for his waistcoat.

"By all means."

"I may know of the way you comport yourself, but no one here will. They would most certainly believe her to be your mistress if you wanted them to."

"Are you suggesting we pretend to be lovers?"

Fogg shrugged slowly. "It would be a way of preventing a lot of questions about who she is and where she came from. Your servants are hardly going to question the unwed master bringing along his mistress, especially considering you had her installed right next door. Not to mention, from what you've said of your father, it would help to uphold the pretense that you are your father's son."

Ash closed his eyes. He had spent a lifetime trying to convince himself that he wasn't like his father. Fogg stopped the brush he was running over Ash's coat and placed a hand on his shoulder.

"You're not him, Ash. It's just a role you're playing right now. I know that."

"I wouldn't be so sure." Steel edged his voice as he spoke, self-hatred oozing through his every pore.

Fogg sighed and shook his head.

"You think I'm better than him, but I'm not. I have

rules now, but back then I didn't. I tupped all the female servants. Sure, I didn't physically force myself on any of them, but once my brother was gone and I was the heir to the earldom, they would hardly have said no. All it took was a wink or a nod and they'd drop to their knees and pleasure me wherever I stood, or allow me to bend them over the nearest piece of furniture.

"You were a boy, Ash. How could you possibly have known it was wrong when that's all you had ever experienced?"

Ash met Fogg's gaze in the mirror. "Don't you dare to make excuses for what I did to those women."

Fogg stepped back and set the brush down firmly. "No. I'm sorry, Ash. You're my employer, but I also count you as my friend, and I will not hold my tongue this time. You are not that man. You've spent a lifetime trying to atone. How many good deeds will be enough? How many people will you have to save? How many times will you have to abide by your own ridiculous rules to realize you are, in fact, a good man?"

Ash turned to face his valet. "Good men don't need rules to be good."

"That's my point, Ash. Neither do you."

Ash simply shook his head.

Fogg let out a defeated sigh. "How long will you need to fetch your new valet?"

"It's early yet, I'll go speak with him today. The

sooner you get other people working, the sooner I can get some answers and leave this godforsaken place."

"How confident are you that he'll say yes?"

"I'll convince him. It's probably best if you go today. Warwick is sure to turn up soon."

Fogg nodded. "I'm kind of surprised he hasn't yet. I assume the storm prevented whoever is working with him from immediately sending word of your arrival."

"I'm sure you're right. Gwen is going to need a new wardrobe, assuming she agrees to this ridiculous plot. I'll take her with me and get that sorted, as well. She'll be safe, so you can go ahead and go, whenever you're ready."

Fogg nodded.

"You will be back, right? I haven't scared you off?"

Amusement flickered in Fogg's eyes. "You're going to have to try a lot harder than that to scare me off. Have you forgotten I'm one of the many lost souls you've saved?"

Ash rolled his eyes, but then he looked at Fogg in earnest. "Thank you, Fogg."

Ash steeled himself for the most difficult challenge of all of this, controlling his demons around Gwen. He checked his reflection one last time. "Wish me luck," he said to Fogg as he turned for the door that led to her rooms.

FOUR

Gwen stared out the window. She could hardly fathom the vastness of this estate. Of Ash's estate. Lord Ashdown, she corrected. It was such a contradiction to everything she knew of him. Sure, he'd always been powerful, but he'd also been kinder than anyone she'd ever known.

As if he'd been summoned by her thoughts, Ash appeared in the doorway that led from her dressing room. He leaned against the jamb, one foot crossed over the other with both hands resting on top of his cane, groomed and dressed to perfection. Warmth filled his eyes, and he smiled. He was still Ash, just as she'd remembered him, except that there was a weariness there that didn't used to be.

"May I come in?" he asked.

"Of course, my lord."

He nodded his approval. "Thank you, Mrs. Lawrence." He leaned on his cane slightly as he made his way across the room. Another change. The cane used to simply swing at his side as he walked.

"Have a seat." He waved the cane toward the chairs near the fireplace. She settled herself into one and he took the other.

"I realize you don't owe me an explanation," she said, "but I would appreciate one. I've never seen you treat anyone the way you treated those servants this morning, and I confess to being a bit startled by it."

He nodded. "I'm sorry. I should have warned you before we got here. Thank you for just going along with it."

She waited for him to continue, but he didn't. "That's not exactly an explanation, Ash."

He sighed and picked a piece of lint from the arm of the chair. "There are some things going on here that I need to get to the bottom of. I need my staff to be nervous because they are more likely to make mistakes so I can figure out which of them are involved. None of them knows what I'm really like, so I'm just acting as my father might have."

"But, presumably, after this long, most of them won't have known your father either."

He chuckled cynically. "Oh, they will have heard stories."

"Was your father so different from you?"

His head whipped around, his brows furrowed. "I can only hope I'm different than he was." His voice was quiet, but she could still hear the anguish in it. Apparently, she'd touched a sore spot.

"I only meant that I've never known you to be anything other than kind. Was your father unkind?"

He barked a scornful laugh. "More than you could possibly imagine." Sadness filled his eyes and he looked down at his lap.

"I'm sorry, Ash. I didn't mean to bring up unpleasant memories."

He raised his gaze to hers, his smile back in place but not quite reaching his eyes. "What have I said about apologizing to me?"

"Yes, my lord," she said in as brattish of a tone as she could manage. A flash of amusement crossed his face and he chuckled.

"I need your help, Gwen, and so I have a proposition for you. I feel as if I should apologize for what I'm about to say before even uttering the words, but here they are anyway. How would you feel about pretending to be my mistress while we're staying here?" He said the words in a nervous rush, as if he were terrified of her response.

"Ash, I've already offered to be your actual mistress. How can you possibly think to shock me by asking me to pretend?"

"I promise to remain a gentleman and not do anything untoward."

She rolled her eyes. "Of course you do."

"In exchange for your acting skills, I will provide you with a new wardrobe and anything else required, as well as pay you for your time."

"Ash," she said, shaking her head. "Can't you ever just let someone help you?"

He ignored her question. "Are you sure, Gwen? I don't want you to do it if you're uncomfortable with any of it."

"Of course I'm sure, Ash. I'm happy to do or be anything you need."

He reached across for her hand and squeezed it. "Thank you. Let's have something to eat, and then we'll head into town. Lord Ashdown's mistress would never be seen in a flour sack of a dress like that one."

"Well, I wouldn't want to disappoint his lordship."

He squeezed her hand again before getting to his feet. "Well then, Mrs. Lawrence, shall we?" He held out his arm and she allowed him to lead her from the room. She would gladly play the role of his mistress if it meant spending more time with him. Her stomach clenched as they made their way toward the dining room. What did that say about her? Until yesterday, she'd thought herself married. She'd made vows. Yet here she was, eagerly anticipating her time with another man.

Was Greg out looking for her even now?

Ash looked down at her hand, which she'd gripped tightly onto his arm without even realizing it. He leaned in and pressed a kiss to her temple, then whispered into her ear.

"I promise we'll talk about whatever this is, as soon as we're alone." He trailed his finger down her neck and along her shoulder, drawing out a shiver, even though she knew the caress was only for the benefit of the watching servants.

He escorted her to the chair to the left of his before seating himself at the head of the table. He ignored every servant that approached, but Gwen saw their trepidation.

Ash picked up a grape and held it to her lips. A flutter of excitement hummed through her as she took it between her teeth, his fingertips just brushing her lips as they closed around the fruit. Somehow, when he'd asked her to pretend to be his mistress, she'd only taken that to mean she'd not deny it. She hadn't realized there'd be this kind of interaction involved. Ash had never so much as flirted with her in all the time she'd lived at Raven House. She, on the other hand, had never ceased flirting with him. She'd taken pleasure in watching him squirm. Perhaps he was paying her back for that now. Well, two could play at that game.

She slipped her hand under the table and placed it on his knee. His pupils dilated as she slid it slowly up his thigh and his throat worked with a swallow. His eyes narrowed in warning, but she simply quirked up a brow, daring him to stop her. The fabric of his trousers tightened beneath her fingers as his arousal grew and she felt a moment of triumph.

But then panic flashed in his eyes.

She quickly moved her hand, placing it over his own on top of the table, squeezing her apology.

She could hear the words as the corners of his eyes crinkled with a small smile, 'you don't have to apologize to me', but she squeezed again to say, 'yes I do'. She'd never intended to make him uncomfortable. Well, perhaps she had a little, but seeing fear in his eyes made her heart hurt for him. He was so strong, it was hard to imagine him scared of anything. Maybe there was more behind his rules than she realized.

When they climbed into his carriage a short time later, he sat down next to her and wrapped his arm around her shoulders, but as soon as the door was shut, he closed the curtains and moved to the opposite seat, taking his warmth with him.

"I'm so sorry, Gwen. If you're too uncomfortable, we can stop. Perhaps I can escort you down to London and come back on my own, once you're safely settled at Raven House."

"Stop it, Ash. I'm not the one who is uncomfortable."

He tipped his head. "Your hand that clamped onto my arm earlier would suggest otherwise."

"That was different." She shook her head. "My thoughts in that moment weren't even about you."

"What were they about, then?"

She folded her arms across her chest. "I will tell you, but only if you promise to answer my questions, as well. And not with your usual dodges. If you're going to expect honesty from me, I deserve the same in return." She wanted to know more about what he was doing here and why he'd stayed away so long.

He nodded, seeming to mull over her words. "Fair enough."

"Promise me, Ash. And promise you won't try to weasel your way around what I'm asking. I know you."

He took her hand in his and looked into her eyes. "I promise." He sat back in his seat, resting his cane on his lap. "So tell me, if it wasn't me, then what had you frightened, Gwen?"

Her heart began to pound again as her mind brought up the question. "What if he's looking for me?" Her fingers fidgeted with the fabric of her skirt.

"You don't need to be afraid, Gwen. You're with me now. I will never let him hurt you again." A muscle ticked in his jaw, and she didn't doubt for a second that he would protect her.

"But what of my wedding vows?"

He let out a sad sigh. "I'm sorry, Gwen, but they weren't real."

"Yes, but I didn't know that. I threw myself at you, quite literally, and didn't feel an ounce of shame when you had your hands wrapped around my bare backside. In fact, I quite enjoyed it. What kind of person does that make me?"

"Gwen, you haven't done anything wrong. You were scared and hurt and not at all in your right mind last night. You certainly don't need to feel guilty about anything you've done. You are a sweet, wonderful, caring woman who was taken advantage of by a terrible man. I wish I could take that away and make it so it never happened."

That wasn't exactly an answer to what she'd asked, but he was right about her state of mind. She simply nodded. "Thank you, Ash, for always being so kind."

Before she could ask more questions, they arrived in the village. She'd never been so spoiled in all her life. By the time they finished, she had several gowns, a new coat, undergarments, shoes, stockings, reticule, night clothes, and multiple pieces of expensive jewelry. She could only imagine how much it had cost him.

"Perhaps not as good as what Ella would have made for you in London," he said, once they were settled into the carriage, once more, "but it will do for the time being. It also allowed me to give some patronage to my own village for once."

"Ash, how am I ever going to pay you back for all of this?"

He waved a hand dismissively. "I told you, it's part of the ruse. You needed appropriate attire."

She shook her head. There was no use arguing with him. "Well then, thank you, my lord."

"You're quite welcome, Mrs. Lawrence."

She giggled. "Where did that name come from anyway?"

He shrugged. "I hadn't thought it through and it was the first thing that popped into my head."

Gwen loved his smile. Especially the mischievous one that made his dark eyes sparkle. She could lose herself in those eyes forever.

"I hope you won't mind." His voice startled her from her dreamy thoughts. "There is another stop I need to make before we return... home." The pause hadn't been lost on her. She knew he didn't think of this place as home and had struggled to say it.

"Of course. Whatever you need."

———

A wave of nervousness washed over Ash as the carriage came to a halt before a small, but well-kept cottage. He asked Gwen to wait and climbed down from the carriage. It was such a complicated mix of emotions that filled him as he approached the front door. He wasn't afraid of the man, even though he had administered countless beatings on his father's orders. Ash hadn't understood at the time, of course, but he could remember the look on

Benson's face. The man had done it in order to spare him from worse.

His hand trembled slightly as he raised it to knock. The door opened, and when Benson's eyes came to rest on Ash's face, his bright smile instantly vanished, replaced by a look of shock, or perhaps even horror. Ash didn't say anything for a moment, allowing him time to simply absorb who it was standing before him.

"My lord!" he finally said, dropping into a deep bow. Confusion and fear had both crossed the man's face, but he didn't meet Ash's gaze again. "To what do I owe the pleasure?"

"Well, it would seem I'm temporarily in need of a valet," Ash said simply.

Benson did look up then, his eyes searching Ash's face. "I don't understand, my lord. Why me?"

Ash shrugged. "Because I believe I can trust you."

Benson scoffed, but then stopped himself. "Apologies, my lord."

"You may speak freely with me, Benson." Ash spoke softly and tried to be as unintimidating as possible.

The older man looked into Ash's eyes, his own beginning to shimmer with unshed tears. "After all I did to you? All the pain I inflicted upon your young body? How could you ever begin to trust me?"

Ash breathed in deeply before responding. "Because I'm not that boy anymore, and I understand now that what you did was, in fact, a kindness. You spared me from the worst of my father's wrath. My father was the brutal tyrant, Benson. Not you."

"But then I abandoned you." Tears spilled over the man's cheeks and his chin trembled.

"Of course you didn't." Ash tried his best to reassure the man. His heart broke for him. He'd had no idea he harbored so much guilt. "After my brother... well, after he was gone, things became volatile. My father's grip on reality was fragile at best, and his rages became indomitable. You couldn't have tempered him, even if you'd stayed."

Benson sniffed. "I would be honored to serve you, my lord." He bent into another deep bow.

Ash placed a hand on his shoulder and urged him upright. "I'll not have you kissing my ring, Benson. I'm not my father."

Benson looked into his eyes, the corners of his mouth tipping up ever so slightly. "Of course you're not, master Adrian."

Joy warmed Ash's heart, healing a small part of it that had broken a lifetime ago. He patted Benson on the shoulder. "Good man. I should warn you, though. You may see me behaving a bit like my father. I'd appreciate it if you would play along. There are things afoot at Woodburn that I'm trying to get to the bottom of. Which is also why I need you to start today. I'll see to anything you might need to make that happen."

Benson's laugh was filled with amusement as he

wiped his tears. "You weren't going to take no for an answer when you came here, were you?"

Ash leaned in and spoke conspiratorially, "I think you'll find I rarely do."

FIVE

N
ot surprisingly, Warwick was waiting for Ash upon his return. He'd known his manager would appear eventually.

"Ah, my lord, so good to see you! You should have sent word you were coming, so I could have had the house made ready for your arrival."

The man had been hired by his father, and Ash had hardly met him before he'd left all those years ago. With his greasy hair parted unflatteringly in the center, his thin eyebrows, and too-long mustache that nearly touched his bottom lip, he could never have been anything but a traitorous snake. But Ash tamped down his fury at the man and kept his face neutral.

"It was a spur of the moment decision."

He turned to Gwen. "Darling, why don't you go up to

your rooms and rest? You must be exhausted after all that shopping. I'll be up shortly."

"Yes, my lord." She played her part to perfection, batting her eyelashes and giggling when he patted her bottom as she walked away. Oh, that bottom of hers. He didn't have to pretend his attraction as he watched it sway all the way up the stairs.

This was a dangerous game he was playing with her.

Ash looked at Warwick, whose eyes were still focused on the top of the stairs where she'd disappeared. It took all his control not to throttle the man. How dare he look at Gwen that way? Ash cleared his throat and Warwick finally tore his gaze away. The lecher didn't even have the decency to look guilty.

"Did you come for any specific reason, my lord?" he asked.

Ash gestured toward the stairs with his chin. "Mrs. Lawrence wanted to get away from London. I thought perhaps the scenery here at Woodburn might make her happy." He flashed a grin the lascivious Mr. Warwick would understand. The knowing gleam in his eyes filled Ash with loathing. He did not like playing nice with this knave.

"Do you have any questions about the estate, my lord? Or perhaps you'd like to see some of the recent improvements?"

"Isn't that what I pay you for? So I don't have to worry about those things?"

"Yes, my lord. Of course."

"You've been overseeing this estate for a long time, Warwick. I'm sure you have it all in hand."

Warwick let out a telltale sigh as Ash watched relief wash over him. He wanted to demand an explanation, confront him with his suspicions, but he had to wait. Fogg would return, and hopefully he'd soon have answers. For now, Ash would have to bite his tongue and bide his time.

"Would you like to dine with us, Warwick?"

"I'd be delighted to, my lord."

"Good. By the time I freshen up a bit, it should be about time. Help yourself to a drink while you wait."

"Thank you, my lord."

A short time later, Ash escorted Gwen into the dining room.

"Warwick, allow me to introduce Mrs. Lawrence. Darling, this is Mr. Warwick, my estate manager."

"A pleasure, Mrs. Lawrence." The man pressed his lips to Gwen's knuckles and Ash's hackles rose when he lingered far too long.

"You must be very good, Mr. Warwick, to manage an estate as impressive as Woodburn Hall."

The man sputtered a bit, feigning humility. "I do my best for his lordship." Did he just wink at her? Ash barely contained the growl that tried to tear its way up his throat.

"Surely, you're just being modest." Gwen touched the man's arm playfully.

She was just being friendly. Playing her role, as he'd asked her to do. Ash had to continue to tell himself that over and over throughout the meal. Each time she laughed at something that scoundrel said or complimented him in some way, it burrowed a little further under Ash's skin. By the time they finished eating, he was digging his fingers into his own leg to stop himself from allowing his anger to show on his face.

Finally, when Ash couldn't handle any more, he pushed himself to his feet. "I hope you'll excuse me, Warwick, but I believe I'll pass on port. Mrs. Lawrence and I will be turning in early tonight."

"Of course," he said, throwing back the last of his wine. "I understand the pair of you were caught out in the storm last night. I'm sure you're eager to sleep in a warm bed tonight."

Ash didn't miss the innuendo in the man's words. "Eager, indeed."

"I'll bid you goodnight, then, Mrs. Lawrence. I hope to see you again soon."

"It was a pleasure meeting you, Mr. Warwick."

The truth was, Gwen had been incredible. She'd put Warwick at ease in a way Ash never would have been able to do on his own. But as he escorted her to her rooms, he couldn't help but ask himself whether he was being protective of her or possessive. He had no business being possessive, as she wasn't his to possess. And yet, there was at least a part of him that longed for her to be. That was the part of himself he had to contain at all costs.

Mary was just warming Gwen's bed when they entered. "My lord." She curtseyed and waited to see if he wanted her to stay or go.

He ignored her and instead spoke to Gwen. "Sleep well," he said, squeezing her hand.

"What? No goodnight kiss?" She pouted her lips, putting on a show for the maid. The little minx had trapped him. Laughter danced in her eyes as he struggled. She knew exactly what she was doing. She'd always been a tease, even when she was at Raven House. He couldn't very well *not* kiss her or the entire household would hear about it before he even drifted off to sleep.

He tugged her hand, pulling her in against him. "I wouldn't dream of depriving you of it, my dear." One didn't kiss one's mistress chastely, so he didn't start slow or gentle. He claimed her mouth roughly, wrapping his hand in a firm grip around her nape. An unexpected explosion of desire rocked him. Parting his lips, he hungrily devoured her mouth. It quickly became apparent that she didn't have much experience in kissing such as this, but he couldn't just stop. He had to see it to its end now. Arousal bloomed as he traced her lips with his tongue. She gasped, and he plunged his tongue into her mouth, tasting the wine she'd drunk with dinner. My

God, it was like heaven. She whimpered quietly and he slowly pulled himself away. Dazed desire clouded her eyes as she looked up at him, her chest heaving with rapid breaths. Her hands were clamped onto his shoulders and she swallowed.

"Goodnight," he said, and pressed a soft kiss to her forehead. He had to get away from her before he lost all control. He strode through her dressing room and into his own. He closed the door and leaned back against the wooden surface. His cane nearly fell out of his shaking fingers. What was he doing? This wasn't right. She hadn't known what she'd signed herself up for, teasing him about a goodnight kiss. And how had she been married for a year and never been kissed properly? Christ. At least she hadn't been afraid. Her whimper had been one of longing, not alarm. That sweet sound would undoubtedly haunt him for the rest of his days.

Benson entered the dressing room from Ash's bedroom. A smile lit his face when he saw Ash, and he bowed. "Good evening, my lord."

It was just the distraction he needed. He slid his mask of calm restraint back into place. "I'm glad you made it, Benson."

"I'm pleased to be here, my lord. Are you ready to prepare for bed?"

Ash nodded and moved to the center of the room where Benson could help him to undress. He forced his thoughts away from Gwen. Or, at least, he tried to. It seemed to be a losing battle.

When Benson removed his shirt, he sucked in a gasp. Ash turned to see him two steps back, a hand to his chest, mouth agape. He'd grown so used to the scars across his back, he forgot just how disturbing they might be to look at. And of course, most of them weren't there when Benson had been thrown out all those years ago. When Benson had gone, his father had taken over the beatings himself. He'd had a leather strap he liked to wield, but would often just use whatever was to hand, and had no compunction about scars or long term damage to Ash's body. Not uncommonly his implement of choice was the cane that Ash still carried to this day. His constant reminder of what he strove not to be.

"My God," Benson uttered. "I'm so sorry, my dear boy."

Ash placed a hand on the man's shoulder. "None of this is your fault, Benson. And as you can see, the wounds have all healed. I'm no longer the frightened boy I was."

"But if I'd just continued to do as he'd demanded, perhaps I could have spared you some of what must have been unbearable agony."

Ash shook his head. "At what cost to your soul? Besides, as I said before, there was no stopping him. He was a monster and we all suffered at his hand, including you."

Benson nodded, but guilt still filled his watery eyes.

"Benson, you did the best you could in a horrific situation, and in case I haven't been clear enough, I forgive you."

Benson closed his eyes and stood silently for a long moment before exhaling a long, shaky sigh. "Thank you, my lord. I'm glad you're here now, a man deserving of this title."

"Well, I don't know about that. We both know the title was never meant to be mine, but I'm glad the brute died anyway. It's just unfortunate I was too much of a coward to help him on his way before he caused so much damage."

He had tried to stand up to his father one time, when he was just fourteen years old. In his resulting tirade, the man had beaten his mother to death. Ash never again failed to submit to him after that day, even after he was grown and could easily have overpowered him.

Cold seeped through his body as the images of his mother's battered face flashed through his mind. If only there was a way to erase them for good. Reliving that horrible event would certainly never bring her back. Not that he missed her. He'd hardly ever seen her as a child, but she still deserved so much better than what she'd endured. No one deserved that.

The warmth of Benson's hand on his bare shoulder brought him out his nightmarish daydream.

"You did the best you could, my boy." Benson quickly

shook his head. "Apologies, my lord. I should not address you so."

Ash smiled approvingly. "You most certainly should. Just not around any of the other staff. At least, not for now. Hopefully I'll be able to wrap up this dreadful business quickly so I can put this whole charade to rest."

———

Gwen had tried her best to hide just how affected she'd been by that kiss while Mary was around, but now that the maid was gone and she lay awake in her bed, she pressed her fingertips to her sensitive lips. They were swollen and still tingled from his touch. No one had ever kissed her like that before. She hadn't even known such a thing was possible. Her nipples grew hard as she remembered the feel of Ash's tongue plunging into her mouth. Why did her body long for him?

Gwen had always submitted to Greg and allowed him the use of her body. He was her husband, after all. Or, at least, she'd believed him to be. Over time, the act had become less painful, but she'd never felt a desire for it. In recent months, it had only ever followed punishment, so the act itself had begun to feel like a punishment. More often than not, he'd simply pushed himself into her body while she was still bent over his desk and then sent her away as soon as he'd finished. She couldn't envision Ash ever doing that. For some reason, she even imagined she might enjoy the act with him. She certainly had enjoyed that kiss. He obviously hadn't been happy about being forced into it, but didn't seem to dislike the kiss itself. Perhaps she could find another way of convincing him to do it again.

Gwen's mind continued to relive every second of that kiss, over and over again, refusing to let her sleep. She didn't mind, but it was making her body feel things she'd never before experienced. Warmth grew in her belly and between her thighs. What did it mean?

A shout tore her from her wanton thoughts. She sat up, staring into the darkness. Another muffled groan sounded through the silence. It had to be Ash. Gwen pushed the blankets aside and climbed out of the bed. She crept through her dressing room to the adjoining door. Sporadic sounds still issued from the other side, so she tapped quietly.

"My lord?" she said, in case there was a servant on the other side of the door, but there was no response.

"No!"

The shout startled her. She opened the door slowly and was met with continued darkness. Carefully, she moved across his dressing room, feeling her way around unfamiliar obstacles. Fortunately, once she reached his bedroom, dying embers in the fireplace and the moonlight that sneaked in around the curtains provided enough light to make out his shape on the bed.

He thrashed, throwing his arm out across the pillow.

"No! Please!" His voice was tortured. "Please no! I'm sorry! Please!" The sound of his desperate anguish made her heart pound.

Gwen rushed to the bed and grabbed hold of his hand. "Ash," she whispered, but he didn't respond and only fought harder, ripping his hand out of her grasp.

She tried again to grab his hand, but he was flailing violently. Finally, out of desperation, she threw herself on top of him and yelled, "Ash!"

He sat bolt upright, and she flung her arms around him to keep from toppling over backwards. "It's alright, Ash. It's just a dream. It was a dream, Ash. I'm here."

His entire body quaked. "Gwen?"

"Yes, Ash. I'm here. It was only a dream." She could feel countless ridges beneath her palm as she rubbed the bare skin of his back. She didn't want to think about what they probably were. The source of the nightmare, no doubt.

He gently pushed her back. "You can't be here, Gwen." Sweat glistened on his skin in the dim light.

"Hush, Ash." She wrapped her arms around him, once more, and planted herself more firmly in his lap.

"You need to go, Gwen. This isn't—"

"I said hush."

He continued to shake, his breathing labored, but he didn't push her away again. After a time, he slowly wrapped his arms around her and simply held her. His warmth easily permeated the thin cotton of her nightgown, and his spicy scent filled her nostrils. She rubbed a hand over his temple as he settled his head against her shoulder.

Her heart ached. Ash was always so strong, never showing a moment of weakness, always firmly in control of himself and everything around him. These must have been unimaginable horrors to break him, even in his dreams.

They sat unmoving and silent for a very long time. For once, she was providing him strength, support, and comfort. He'd always been the one to save everyone else, and she was so glad that tonight, he was allowing her this.

Slowly, he lifted his head and gazed into her eyes. The shaking had subsided and his breathing had calmed. He looked lost as he stared at her, as if he wasn't sure how to respond to her kindness. As if it were the first time he'd ever been shown any, but that couldn't be. He brushed her hair back and tucked it behind her ear before gently holding her neck. He dropped his forehead softly against hers and closed his eyes, allowing himself a deep breath. It caressed her skin as he exhaled. Gwen would happily stay in this moment forever, with this man, and his warmth and his tenderness.

"Gwen."

"Shhh." She reached between them and touched a finger against his lips. He was going to tell her to leave again, and she wasn't about to abandon him.

He pressed a light kiss against the finger and slowly raised his head. "Thank you." His voice was barely more than a whisper, but she could sense the depth of his gratitude. It came straight from his soul.

You're welcome didn't seem to articulate how she felt, so instead, she took his hand in hers and brought it to her lips. She placed a lingering kiss against the back and breathed in, his alluring scent intoxicating. It brought her a sense of security and safety.

"You need to get some sleep, Gwen. I'm sorry I woke you."

Gwen shook her head. "No."

One corner of his mouth ticked up. "No?"

"No," she repeated.

He chuckled then, and it warmed her to see the pain disappearing from his eyes. "No, what?"

"I'm not leaving you tonight, Ash."

He groaned and dropped his forehead against hers, once more. "You know you can't stay, Gwen. I'm not even dressed, and this is wholly inappropriate."

"I don't care," she said. "I'm not leaving you alone, Ash."

"Gwen." He let out an exasperated sigh. "Are we just going to sit like this all night, then?"

She shrugged. "If that's what you want. Personally, I'd rather get under the blankets where it's warm."

"I don't have anything on under here!" He sounded appalled and she couldn't contain her laughter.

She shrugged again. "It's not as if you haven't seen *me* naked."

"That's different," he argued.

"Listen." She once again placed a finger over his lips, which continued to smile beneath. "I promise to behave myself. I won't touch anything below your waist, and I'll try my best to sleep and not bother you." His eyes grew wider with every word she spoke. "But," she said more loudly, as he tried to interrupt her. "I will not leave you tonight. Even if that means I have to sit just like this until the sun comes up."

He closed his eyes and shook his head. "You may promise those things, but how can you be so sure I will follow suit?"

She cupped his cheek, his stubble grazing against her palm. "Because I know you, Ash. If I say I don't want anything to happen, nothing will happen. Honestly, I could throw back these blankets right now and beg you to take me, and you still wouldn't." He had more self-control than anyone she'd ever met.

After a long moment, he finally nodded. "You are a stubborn little imp." With a sigh, he lifted the blankets beside him. Triumph flooded through her. Not because she had won, but because he was allowing her behind the armor he always wore. He was allowing himself to be vulnerable, even if just for one night. She scurried to climb under the covers before he changed his mind. As he laid back, she snuggled up against his side and he froze, holding his breath for a moment before he slowly relaxed and wrapped his arm around her shoulders. He gasped as she pressed her icy toes against his bare leg.

"Christ, woman. How are they so cold?"

Gwen giggled and snuggled more tightly against him. With her arm thrown over his chest and her head cradled against his shoulder, she felt like she was home. She would gladly have lain awake, enjoying their closeness all night long, but in the safety of his embrace and surrounded by his warmth, sleep claimed her in no time at all.

SIX

How was any of this real? Gwen was asleep in his arms, her body pressed against his, the only barrier between them the thin cotton of her nightgown. And yet, it wasn't lewd or indecent or even tempting him for something that may be. It was the most wholesome, most tender thing he'd ever experienced.

Even as she'd sat in his lap, straddling him, her breasts pressed against his chest, it was her heart he'd craved and not her body. She'd shown him such sweet kindness. No one had ever consoled him like that before, just held him and allowed him to not be strong. Gwen hadn't only allowed it, she'd demanded it of him. She'd seen him in the worst moments of his fear, shaking and sweating from the horrific nightmare, and she hadn't turned away. She hadn't sneered or judged him as lacking in some way. She hadn't asked him to explain or tell her about his dream. Even feeling the scars on his back hadn't caused her to recoil in disgust. She'd simply continued to hold him and soothe him, as if he were the only thing that mattered in that moment.

He breathed in her sweet scent and pressed a light kiss against the top of her head. "Thank you, my angel," he whispered, even though he knew she wouldn't hear it. Eventually, he drifted off for a few hours, her protective presence keeping his nightmares at bay.

When he woke, the room was beginning to lighten. She was still snuggled against his side, but her leg was now thrown over his, and lust was stirring. Carefully, he extricated himself from her embrace and slid out of bed. For a moment, he simply stared down at her precious form. He'd be eternally grateful for the gift she'd given him last night and wanted to seal this image of her in his mind to treasure forever.

He grabbed his cane and quietly left before she woke to see him standing there naked and staring at her like some depraved wolf.

An hour later, Ash chastised himself for being a coward as he rode out across his estate. Somehow, facing Gwen in the daylight, knowing what she'd witnessed, had been too daunting. He'd told Benson to keep an eye on her, and Mary to see that she had everything she needed, and then he'd simply left.

Something in the distance caught his eye. A pair of

men were having a heated discussion. He slowed his
horse and moved carefully into the shadows of a row of
trees. One of them was undoubtedly Warwick, but Ash
didn't recognize the other. From this distance, he could
really only tell that he was tall and lean with dark brown
hair.

Unfortunately, in spite of the pointing and shouting,
Ash couldn't understand a word of their argument. Eventually, the younger man threw his hands up and stormed
away before mounting a chestnut horse and riding in the
opposite direction from where Ash watched. Warwick
mounted his own horse and headed for the house. He
was probably going in search of Ash, but he didn't wish
to see the man just now. Let him wait. He'd undoubtedly
make himself comfortable and help himself to Ash's
liquor.

Ash nudged his horse forward. Perhaps if he hurried,
he could follow the other man and see where he was
headed.

His destination turned out to be a small house on the
estate. He must be one of Ash's tenants. As the man
jumped down from his horse, a young girl, maybe four or
five years old, sprinted out and threw herself into his
waiting arms. She had messy brown curls and an excited
smile. Ash stayed out of sight, but now that he was
closer, he could see that the man was only eighteen or
twenty. Not really old enough to be the girl's father, so

perhaps she was his sister? He set her down and sent her back into the house while he dealt with the horse.

What had he been arguing with Warwick about?

Ash spent a couple more hours out on the estate. He'd been lucky to be in the right place at the right time today, but now, it was time to head back. The cold was making his leg ache, and his stomach was rumbling.

"Is Warwick still here?" Ash asked as he handed off his hat and coat.

"Yes, my lord. In the drawing room, I believe."

"Send in some tea and some kind of food. I'm famished."

"Yes, my lord." The footman hurried off to do his bidding and Ash made his way to the drawing room.

He pushed the door open and strolled in before nearly tripping over his own feet as they lodged in place at the sight that met him. Warwick stood in the middle of the room, his hand resting on the head of a young maid who was on her knees before him. The two sprang apart at his sudden intrusion, Warwick hastily stuffing himself back into his trousers. A simmer of rage instantly rushed through Ash's veins. He would kill the man. To hell with trying to figure out what he'd been doing on the estate.

The maid jumped to her feet, her gaze firmly on the floor and her cheeks as red as apples. It took every ounce of control he had not to fly into a rage, but he needed to make sure she was safe first and then he'd deal with Warwick.

"A word," he said quietly. He didn't know her name so he simply gestured toward the door. When she realized he was addressing her, she darted out of the room.

"I'm sorry, my lord. I didn't mean to do anything wrong. I'm so sorry." Tears sprang from her eyes.

"Did he hurt you?" Ash kept his voice as calm as possible.

She shook her head.

"I want you to go up to the countess's chambers. Find Mrs. Lawrence. Tell her that I sent you and that I want her to stay with you. Do you understand?"

The girl's brow was furrowed and she seemed unable to speak.

"She will see that you're taken care of. Go on." He gave her a little nudge, and with a nod, she hurried off, sobs following in her wake.

Ash finally allowed his fury to rampage fully through him as he entered the drawing room, once more. "How dare you?" he growled as he advanced on Warwick.

The filth held up his hands. "Apologies, my lord. Your father never minded if I had a little fun, so I just assumed—"

Ash didn't let him finish. He slammed his fist into the man's jaw, sending him sprawling onto the floor.

"I am *not* my father." This charade was over. Seething anger coursed through his veins as he stood over the lecherous snake cowering on the floor. He pounded his foot into Warwick's stomach, knocking the wind out of him. "If you ever lay a finger on a woman under my protection again, I will end your life before the sun rises. Do I make myself clear?"

Warwick sputtered and choked, seemingly unable to speak, but he did manage a nod of understanding. Just then, a footman entered with a tea tray, his eyes wide at the ensuing chaos, the contents of the tray rattling.

"Get someone to help you and lock this cretin in a room somewhere so I can deal with him later. Otherwise, I might kill him."

The man appeared to be frozen in place with shock. "Now!" Ash shouted, slamming his cane against the floor.

The footman jumped. "Yes, my lord." He deposited the tray and sprinted from the room.

Ash looked down at Warwick, who was still groaning on the floor, and pressed the end of his cane against his chest. "You'll want to cooperate so I don't have to knock you unconscious."

Warwick finally found his voice. "She was just a maid. Hardly a reason to be upset. I didn't realize you wanted them all to yourself." Ash slammed his foot into Warwick twice more.

"I suggest you stop talking now." A chill hung on the edge of Ash's words and Warwick closed his mouth.

Three footmen entered and hauled him to his feet. "You can't do this, Ashdown," he spat angrily.

"I think you'll see I can, and I will."

They dragged him out of the drawing room, his shouts echoing behind him as they forced him through the house.

Ash poured a glass of brandy and drained it down his throat. For a moment, he'd seen himself standing there where Warwick had been. How many times had he done the same, or worse? With a roar, he hurled the empty glass into the fireplace where it shattered. He dug the heels of his hands against his eyes wishing desperately that he could erase his past. With a weary sigh, he turned to see his butler standing in the doorway looking uncharacteristically ruffled.

"Do you need anything, my lord?"

Ash shook his head slowly. "Thank you, Moulton."

The man was confused by Ash's sudden show of patience. Perhaps this whole plan had been a mistake.

"Of course, my lord," he said slowly. He bowed, and left Ash alone in the drawing room.

———

Gwen may have been disappointed to wake up alone in Ash's bed, but she hadn't been surprised. She also wasn't surprised that he stayed away all day, out on his estate. She didn't expect him to drop what he was doing to entertain her, but she had a feeling he was avoiding her because he was ashamed of the vulnerability he'd displayed last night. Which was ridiculous, of course, but also, not unexpected. Gwen would treasure the night they'd spent together for the rest of her days, never forgetting the warmth of his body against hers or the tenderness of his head resting against her shoulder while she'd comforted him.

She walked to the window for probably the hundredth time hoping to catch a glimpse of him, but still nothing. She had seen Mr. Warwick arrive a couple of hours ago. She had no interest in seeing that man again if she could avoid it. Something about him was oddly familiar, and he made her exceedingly uncomfortable.

A light but frantic tapping sounded at her door.

"Come," she called.

The door opened cautiously and a young maid took a hesitant step into the room. She was obviously distraught.

"Mrs. Lawrence?"

Gwen rushed to her and ushered her inside, closing the door. "Are you hurt?" she asked quickly.

The girl shook her head. Her eyes darted about the room as tears dripped from the corners.

"What's your name?" Gwen asked softly.

"Sandra." She sniffled, her eyes not meeting Gwen's.

"What's wrong, Sandra?"

"His lordship told me to come to your rooms." She looked up then. "He said you'd take care of me."

Gwen's stomach dropped. There was only one reason

Ash would send a maid up to her like this. She wrapped her arms around the girl. "You're safe now, Sandra." The girl's body trembled, but she didn't sob or speak. Probably still in shock from whatever had happened. Gwen got her settled into a chair and poured her a cup of tea.

"It's not very hot anymore, but it will do for now." Gwen certainly didn't want to summon someone. The last thing this girl needed was a witness to what she was going through.

"Thank you." She sipped the tea in silence for a minute. Gwen realized she was hovering, so she seated herself in the empty chair across from Sandra. Slowly the girl looked up at her. "I didn't mean to cause any trouble."

Angry shouts sounded from across the house and Sandra flinched, her eyes growing wide with panic. "It's alright, Sandra. You're safe here." Gwen wasn't able to make out any of the words, and the shouting quickly grew quiet.

"What happened, Sandra?"

"Well." She stared down at her fidgeting thumbs, her pale cheeks growing pink. "Mr. Warwick wanted some company." She swallowed before continuing. "His lordship walked in and—" The words trailed off and she raised her gaze to meet Gwen's. "I've never seen someone look so angry." She nibbled on the corner of her lip. "Is he going to sack me?"

Gwen crouched next to Sandra's chair, taking hold of

one of the girl's hands. "No, Sandra. You haven't done anything wrong. He wasn't angry with you. I promise." Gwen squeezed her hand. "Was this the first time something like that has happened with Mr. Warwick? Or has he asked for that kind of company from you before?"

"It wasn't the first time," Sandra said quietly.

"Nor the second?" Gwen asked. Sandra shook her head. This had been going on regularly. Gwen hooked a finger under the girl's chin to urge her to look at her. "Lord Ashdown is a good man, Sandra, and I can promise you that he will ensure that nothing like that ever happens again."

Her brow furrowed. "Is he staying?"

Gwen shook her head. "I don't believe so, but he'll find someone trustworthy to take over in his absence. Clearly, Mr. Warwick was not the right man."

SEVEN

When Ash entered his chambers, he was shocked but so relieved to see Fogg there. A footman cowered in the chair beside him.

"Thank God you're back, Fogg. I've just mucked everything up."

He raised his brow and turned his hands up exasperatedly. "I've been gone a day and a half. How did you manage that?"

Ash shook his head and gestured at the footman. "What's going on here?"

"Oh him?" Fogg jerked toward him and the man flinched. "He's the one who's been reporting to Warwick since you arrived. I found him in here poking about."

Ash folded his arms across his chest, tucking his cane into the crook of his elbow. He turned his glare on the footman. He was hardly more than a boy and looked terrified. Ash couldn't help but feel a twinge of pity for him. "What's your name?"

"James, my lord." Fear made his voice crack slightly as he spoke.

"You have some explaining to do, James."

He swallowed, but he didn't speak.

"Unless you'd rather I just let you go without a reference. Warwick certainly won't be able to help you, though, as he's currently locked up, so I don't kill the vile bastard."

Fogg swung around to face him. Ash shrugged. "I told you I mucked it up."

"Well, it's good I didn't waste any time, then."

"Did you get some answers?"

Fogg rolled his eyes and gestured to the footman.

"Oh, right," Ash said. He'd been so anxious to hear what Fogg had uncovered, he'd almost forgotten about the footman. "So what's it going to be, James? Are you going to talk or take your chances out in the cold tonight?"

"I'm sorry, my lord. I'll tell you anything. Please don't throw me out."

"Good choice, lad. So what are you doing in my chambers?"

He swallowed and his voice shook as he spoke. "Mr. Warwick wanted me to see if I could find anything that might indicate you have some kind of reason for being here other than just visiting your estate. He said it's too much of a coincidence, you showing up after all this time, right after the robbery."

"And which robbery is that?"

James shrugged timidly. "I don't know. That's just what he said."

"And why did you think you owe your loyalty to him, James, rather than to me? I am, after all, the master of this estate."

He lowered his gaze and picked at the fabric of his trouser leg. "I'm sorry, my lord. I didn't mean to be disloyal."

Ash tapped his cane against the man's knee. "Look at me when you're speaking to me," he barked.

James shrank back in the chair but raised his frightened eyes to Ash's face. "I'm sorry, my lord."

"So if you didn't mean to be disloyal, then explain to me how one is accidentally perfidious."

He started to lower his gaze again but caught himself and quickly corrected. "Mr. Warwick said he'd tell you I stole a bottle of brandy if I didn't do as he asked."

"That doesn't explain why you sent word to him when I arrived."

"Well, the truth is, I did steal a bottle of brandy, six months ago. He's been holding it over my head ever since then, and I thought perhaps that might finally put me in his good graces."

Ash sighed irritably. "Does this job really mean so

little to you that you would throw it away for a bottle of brandy?"

"No. It was stupid and I swear it will never happen again, my lord."

"Do you know anything about a blackmail scheme Warwick is running?"

"Actually," Fogg interjected, "it turns out it isn't really a blackmail scheme."

Ash waited for Fogg to explain, but he didn't. "What is it then?" he finally asked.

"I thought you must have figured that out, since you said you have him locked up."

Ash shook his head. Why was Fogg stalling? "Fogg?"

"You have to promise me you won't kill him, Ash."

"What has he done, Fogg? Does this have something to do with Gwen?"

Fogg nodded slowly, and that was all Ash needed. "I will kill him," he growled as he turned for the door.

Before he even knew something was happening, Fogg somehow managed to tug him backwards, sweep his legs out from under him and push him into the empty chair. His hand was pressed firmly against Ash's chest.

"I can't let you kill him, Ash."

Ash was stunned. Not by the fact that Fogg was physically able to do what he'd done, but by the fact that he had. What had gotten into him?

Fogg turned his head toward James. "If a word of any of what has just happened leaves this room, I will cut out your tongue and send it to your mother. Do you understand?"

The man choked, the color draining from his face. "I understand! I won't say a word! I haven't seen or heard anything."

"Jesus, Fogg. What is wrong with you? You've scared the lad half to death. Now let me up because I am going to kill that bastard."

"You're not, Ash. I'm sorry. He is going to be arrested for what he's done, but if you kill him, it will be you they are arresting, instead. And if you're in prison or hanged, I'm out of a job, so I'm afraid you're going to stay in that chair until you promise not to kill him." He shrugged and lazily swung Ash's cane back and forth at his side.

"I'm not making any promises, Fogg. If he did something to hurt Gwen—" Anger throbbed inside his veins.

"He did," Fogg said quietly. "And if the circumstances were different, you know I'd take care of the body when you were finished, but that just can't happen this time."

"Why not?" Ash raged.

"Because he was already being investigated. This is bigger than just Gwen."

"*Just* Gwen?" His voice trembled as fury and heartache warred within his chest.

"That's not what I meant, Ash. Warwick and his brother and a couple of other men have been providing fake marriages for a price, and they've been doing it for years."

Ash turned his gaze on James. "Did you know anything about that?"

"No, my lord. I would never participate in something so wretched."

"I think perhaps one of my tenants is involved, as well. I saw Warwick and him arguing this morning."

"We'll certainly look into him then," Fogg assured him. "Now, if you didn't know about any of this, why is he locked up somewhere in your house?"

"I walked in on him... with a maid."

"Oh." Fogg cringed slightly. "So when you say he's locked up, it isn't without some injuries."

"Only a black eye and some broken ribs. Now I wish I'd killed him then and there. I had no idea my loyal servant was going to turn on me." He glowered at Fogg.

"I know, Ash. I am sorry. I didn't hurt your leg, did I?"

"Just promise me you won't stop me from killing the man who actually abused her."

"I'll gladly hold him upright until you beat his last breath out of him."

Ash looked over at James. "I bet this wasn't how you thought your day was going to go when you put that livery on this morning, was it?"

James shook his head. "But I can promise that I'll never do anything to put myself on the wrong side of you again."

Ash threw back his head and roared with laughter. And then, using the distraction to his advantage, he surged to his feet, wrapped an arm around Fogg's middle and hurled him into the chair, retrieving his cane in the process. He pressed the end of it roughly into Fogg's chest.

"Don't you ever do something like that to me again." He drew the words out slowly for emphasis. "You seem to have forgotten, Fogg, I didn't build my humble empire by being weak. Or complacent. Or nice."

Fogg held up his hands. "I'm sorry, Ash. I may have overstepped."

"There's no may about it, Fogg. Except that you may be out of a job."

Fogg grunted as Ash shoved the cane against his chest before he turned and left the room.

Ash fumed as he mounted his horse, cursing his sore leg. He wanted to have a conversation with the young tenant before anyone had a chance to stop him. When he arrived, he didn't knock or announce himself in any way, he just stormed straight into the house. The man whipped around, dropping the saucepan he was carrying, which landed with a loud clang, and porridge splattered across the floor.

Panic flashed over the man's face and he shuffled backwards as Ash charged toward him. Ash grabbed the front of the man's shirt in his fist and slammed him against the nearest wall. A high-pitched scream pierced through the room.

"Please don't hurt my brother." Her small, scared

voice wrapped itself around Ash's heart. In his anger, he'd forgotten all about her.

The man he had pinned against the wall swallowed and spoke softly. "Please not in front of her. I swear I won't try to run."

Ash wasn't in the business of terrorizing children. He let go of the man's shirt, then turned and crouched before the little girl. "I'm sorry, Poppet. I didn't mean to frighten you. I just need to have a word with your brother. You stay here where it's warm, and we'll be just outside."

"You promise you won't hurt him?" The girl's wide, innocent eyes could force a promise out of even the meanest thug.

"I promise." With a sigh, he stood and walked out the front door. He heard the man give the girl some reassurance before he stepped out and closed the door behind him.

"Thank you," he said. "And thank you for trying to put her at ease."

Ash grunted. "I'm not a complete monster." The look in the man's eyes said he wasn't so sure about that.

"Do you know who I am?" Ash asked the question in earnest, not pompously trying to put the man in his place.

"Yes, my lord."

"Well then, you have me at a disadvantage, because I don't know who you are."

"Trent Gibson."

"And do you know why I'm here, Trent?"

Trent mulled it over for a moment before answering. "I have a guess."

"I'll make it easy for you. What is your role in the fake marriage scheme?"

The man blanched. "The what?"

"Don't," Ash warned. "I'd really like to keep that promise I made to your sister."

Trent shook his head frantically. "I don't know anything about any fake marriages. I swear."

He seemed genuinely confused about the accusation, but that didn't make sense. "Then why is it you think I'm here?"

He seemed to be debating what he should say.

"Trent, you might as well just be honest while you have a free pass. I promised your sister I wouldn't hurt you, and believe it or not, I am a man of my word."

He gave a resigned shrug. "I assumed you were here to confront me about the robbery."

Ash was beginning to feel like he'd stepped into some sort of pantomime. How did things just continue to surprise him? How the hell was this man involved with the robbery at his club in London? Fogg had tracked down the only man who had gotten away, and this certainly wasn't him.

"What part did you have in the robbery?"

Trent furrowed his brow. He looked almost offended by the question. "I didn't play a part in it. I was the one who made it happen. Apparently, I chose the wrong people for the job, though, since they didn't actually succeed."

"It wouldn't have made any difference. No one tries to rob my club and walks away. But why did you do it? Did you need money so badly?"

He shrugged. "I wanted to take something from you, to hurt you."

"Well, you got what you wanted, then." Ash's voice was escalating. "They bloody shot me! This goddamn leg still hurts!"

"I had heard that, and I'm sorry. They weren't supposed to do that. No one was supposed to get hurt. Not like that."

"So why did you want to hurt me? What did I do to you?"

"Your father gave you everything." Trent was shouting now, emotion making his voice quiver slightly. "Your whole life was just handed to you on a silver platter. The title, the estate, that club where you live a life of excess surrounded by extravagance and whores. He could have at least left my mother something when he died."

Ash had wondered when one of his father's inevitable bastards would eventually show up. He was surprised Trent was the first, honestly.

"All my mother ever wanted was for him to recognize me as his son. Instead, he left us to rot."

Ash laughed cynically as he removed his coat. "Do

you want to know what it looks like to be recognized by *our* father?" He stripped off the rest of his clothing above the waist, the icy breeze biting his skin as he turned around.

Trent gasped at the sight of his mangled back. Ash simply stood, allowing him time to take in every last scar. "You think my life was so easy?" He slid his arms back into his shirt and began closing the buttons. "Well, I think you had a lucky escape, and so did your mother. Our beast of a father beat mine to death." He closed his waistcoat and settled his coat back onto his shoulders. "And my brother, the one who was supposed to inherit all of this, hanged himself to get away from our father. Do you still wish he had recognized you as his son?"

Trent's mouth was agape, and he was clearly at a loss for words so Ash continued. "As for my life of excess— first of all, if you ever again refer to the women who work for me as whores, I will break your jaw." He leaned in, his face barely an inch from Trent's. "Is that clear?"

"Yes," Trent said quietly.

"Most of those women were on the streets before they found their way to me. I give them money, a roof over their head, and skills they can use to have a better life. They dance in my club, fully clothed, and no one is allowed to lay a finger on them. Especially, me." Ash pointed at his own chest. "So what you see as a life of excess, is at least partly, a life of penitence. My attempt to make up for a small fraction of the evil our father, and I, bestowed upon the world."

Trent seemed to shrink right before Ash's eyes. A sadness settled on his features, and perhaps guilt? He was also beginning to tremble from the cold. He hadn't put on a coat before coming outside.

"I'm truly sorry, my lord. I had no idea." He looked into Ash's eyes. "Did he really do all of that?" He gestured toward Ash's back.

Ash let out a long sigh. What the hell was he going to do with this man... who was apparently his half-brother? He didn't seem to be the villain Ash had imagined him to be when he'd set out to confront him. Just a man who was angry and hurting. And rightly so.

"Why don't we finish this conversation inside where it's warm?"

Trent shook his head. "I don't want Maggie to hear about the things I've done." A sad smile twitched on his lips. "She believes I'm a good man. Thinks I hang the stars in the sky." He waved a hand across the sky.

"You still can be, you know."

"Says the man who was shot because of me."

Ash waved that away. "Yes, well. I wish you had just come to me, but I think I understand why you didn't. I'm sorry for what he did to you and your mother, Trent. But I'm not sorry you never knew him."

"Perhaps I'm not either, now that I know. Not that I had much of a chance. I was only three when he died, apparently. My mother always told me stories, though, about my father who was the earl of a grand estate."

"It's not all it's cracked up to be. Just tonight I have a villain locked up in my house waiting to be arrested, a maid who he"—Ash paused and swallowed down the rage that rose in his throat—"will never touch again, that I need to make sure is taken care of, an entire household of women who may have also been abused by him, some kind of fake marriage scheme that involved someone I failed at protecting, a disloyal footman locked in my bedchamber, the woman I failed to protect once, and have to figure out how to be more successful with this time around, an estate that no longer has a manager, and apparently, a half-brother I never knew existed."

Trent blinked. "Jesus."

Suddenly, laughter surged out of him. What else could he possibly do? Eventually, Trent began to laugh as well. None of it was funny, but the sheer amount of chaos was utterly preposterous and seemed to have knocked his senses loose.

"I know this is probably a stupid question," Trent said after a moment, "but is there anything I can do to help?"

"You can tell me anything you know about Warwick. I saw you arguing with him this morning, so the two of you obviously have some kind of connection."

"We were arguing about you, actually. He's upset because he believes you came here because of my failed robbery. But he doesn't like me, regardless. I've been kind of blackmailing him. Basically, he would report repairs as more serious than they were. I would do the work, and he would pay me more than it was worth."

Ash nodded. "That makes sense. That was the original reason I came here. The books had been getting more and more suspicious over the past year."

"I'm sorry, my lord. I don't have the money to pay you back, but I'll work it off any way I can."

"Don't be ridiculous, of course you won't." Ash didn't care about the money. At least, not now that he was beginning to understand the reasons behind the theft. Trent undoubtedly needed it to take care of his sister. He hadn't been making her porridge for supper because it was her favorite. He was barely getting by. "But I don't understand. How were you blackmailing Warwick if you didn't know about the fake marriages?"

Trent shrugged. "It started as just a bluff, really. I saw how he carried himself around this estate, how he treated people. I know his type. There was no way he wasn't stealing from you one way or another. So I just said I had proof of his wrongdoing and threatened to send it to you if he didn't agree to my demands. In addition to the repairs, he also told me about your club."

Trent was clever and resourceful, and seemed to want to be good when it came down to it. There was certainly no doubt he loved his sister.

"Thank you for your honesty, Trent. Come and see me tomorrow. We have more to discuss, but you're freezing, and I have a veritable circus that I need to get back to."

Ash reached into his pocket, pulled a handful of bank notes out of his clip, and pressed the folded paper into Trent's palm.

His eyes grew wide. "My lord, I can't take this."

"It's Ash, and I'm not giving you a choice. I'd like to come in and have a quick word with Maggie before I leave, if you'll allow it."

He hesitated a moment, his eyes trying to read Ash's intentions.

"I won't do anything to hurt her, Trent."

He nodded and opened the door. Maggie looked her brother over from head to toe. "You kept your promise?" she asked shyly.

"Of course I did." Ash crouched down again. "I always keep my promises."

"Maggie, this is Lord—"

"Tsst." Ash cut him off before he could finish. "I'm Uncle Ash. It's nice to meet you, Maggie." Not a chance in Hades was he going to have this sweet, innocent girl calling him Lord Ashdown.

She looked to her brother, unsure of what to make of Ash. Trent nodded and Ash was quite sure he brushed a tear from the corner of his eye.

"Your brother is going to take you into the village for some sweets tomorrow."

"He is?" Her face split with a wide grin and she

danced in a little circle.

Ash nodded. "And if you're good, he might even get you something special like a toy or a new dress."

Her mouth fell open as she gazed up at her brother, completely in awe of him. Somehow, this little girl he hadn't even known existed yesterday had just charmed her way right into his heart. The dark, ambitious, scowling, sinister, club-owning, fear-inspiring ruler of Raven Row, had been brought low by a slip of a girl with chestnut curls that bounced when she danced and a smile that could light up the darkest of nights. Ash would do whatever he could to make sure that her brother... his brother... could always be exactly the man she believed him to be right now, in this magical moment.

Ash pushed himself up with his cane and walked with Trent to the door. "I don't know how to thank you, my l... Ash."

"You can thank me by bringing her with you when you come up to the house tomorrow, so she can show me her special treats."

"You're going to spoil her. We can't usually afford sweets and things."

"You can now, and of course I'm going to spoil her. That's what uncles are supposed to do, isn't it?"

Ash could see Trent struggling with accepting kindness from him. He placed a hand on the man's shoulder. "We'll talk tomorrow. Rest easy tonight."

Ash knew the look that filled Trent's eyes. It was the

look of someone who'd just had their whole view of the world turned on its head. He'd obviously only ever been able to trust himself, and therefore, didn't trust any of this yet. But he would, in time.

"Wish me luck!" Ash called as he climbed into the saddle. Despite the chaos he was riding back to, his heart felt lighter than it had since he arrived.

EIGHT

Gwen had heard Ash's valet leave him at least a half hour ago, but still, he hadn't paid her a visit. There had obviously been plenty keeping him busy during the day, but why was he still avoiding her? She thought he'd at least want to talk to her about the maid he'd sent up earlier, even if Mrs. Archer had eventually come to collect her.

She had no right to expect him to keep her company and entertain her. He'd already done so much for her, she should just leave him be, and yet, her feet were carrying her toward the door to his chambers. Even to her, this place felt a bit like a mausoleum, and she longed for his company.

As she carefully pushed the door open, she told herself she wasn't knocking just in case he was asleep and she didn't want to wake him. But in truth, she didn't want to give him a chance to refuse her.

Ash sat in one of the plush chairs before the fire, a glass of brandy in his hand. He wore pajama bottoms, but on top, only his robe and it was wide open. Firelight danced across his bare chest, and she drank it in for far too long before raising her gaze to his eyes, which were watching her.

"Good evening, Gwen." To her disappointment, he pulled the sides of his robe closed. "You should be asleep."

She shrugged and padded further into the room, silently begging him not to send her away. "I missed you."

"I'm sorry. I was..." He let out a long sigh. "I had a lot on my plate today."

He set down his glass and held out a hand to her. Her heart leapt at the invitation. He wasn't sending her away. At least, not yet. She practically skipped across the room to him. She closed her eyes, reveling in his warmth as his strong fingers surrounded her hand.

"I want to thank you, Gwen."

"For what?"

"So many things." His smile held such kindness. "Let's start with the easiest ones."

"Oh, well if there's a list, then I'd better settle in." He sucked in a breath as she climbed onto his lap. Holding it in, he closed his eyes, every muscle in his body tense. She knew it was a risk and he might send her away, but she desperately needed to feel his warmth, to be close to him. After a moment, he slowly blew out the breath he was holding, and opened his eyes. He gave a little nod, seemingly to himself.

"You're sitting in my lap, Gwen."

She bit down on her lip to stop the laughter threatening to burst out of her. "Am I?" She looked about in feigned surprise.

He chuckled. "You are an imp."

"My feet are cold. I couldn't very well just stand there."

"Well, we can't have that." He wrapped his hand around her icy toes, on top of his thigh, sending a delicious warmth through her entire body.

"So, you were saying?" she prompted.

Ash's purr of laughter made heat bloom in her belly. Why did he affect her so?

"Thank you for taking care of that maid today. I knew you'd be just what she needed in that moment."

"Thank you, Ash, for trusting me enough to send her up to me. For trusting that I wouldn't need any explanation."

"Of course I knew you'd take care of her. You're an angel, Gwen." His hand gently massaged her foot. He probably wasn't even aware that he was doing it, but she certainly was. It stirred more life into the strange longing that was beginning to course through her veins. "Last night, you were my angel. That's really what I wanted to thank you for." He reached his arm around her and eased her down to rest her head on his shoulder. "You saved me from my nightmares, and although I'm sorry you had to see me in that state, I will never forget the kindness you showed me. No one has ever done anything like that for me before, and I'm not sure what I did to deserve it."

Gwen sat up and cupped his cheek. "You really can't see your own kindness, can you? Ash, you saved me after I tried to steal from you. You didn't stop to consider whether or not I was deserving of your kindness. You simply gave it. So why do you believe you have to earn kindness from others?"

"I—" He opened his mouth and closed it, and for a long moment his thoughts turned inward. After a bit, he lowered his forehead to rest against hers. She liked it when he did that. "I have a lot to atone for, Gwen, but I don't want to talk about that tonight."

She wouldn't press the issue. "Well, there is something we could do that doesn't involve talking." She paused for a moment, nervousness fluttering in her stomach. "I was hoping, if I asked nicely, you might kiss me again." Gwen's heart pounded inside her chest as she waited for his answer.

"Oh, Gwen. You know I have strict rules about that kind of thing. As your employer, it isn't right for me to engage in such things with you."

She wasn't going to point out that she was currently

sitting in his lap while he rubbed her bare feet, or that she'd slept against his naked body the previous night. "Hear me out. After my last experience, I don't think I ever want to marry again, so perhaps we can stretch a few of the rules, just until we return to London. Once we get back to Raven House, I promise I won't ask for anything that's forbidden."

His eyes filled with such tenderness as he gently brushed his hands over her hair before settling them against her neck. Slowly, he pulled her closer and pressed his lips against her forehead. She was about to complain that that wasn't what she'd meant, but he didn't stop there. His lips were so soothing as he pressed featherlight kisses between her brows, over her eyes, and across her cheeks.

Her lips tingled with anticipation before he even touched them. When he finally did, a burst of longing swept through her, and she immediately opened for him, but he didn't plunge inside as he had the night before.

Strangely, his leisurely pace stirred desire in her even more than the passionate kiss from last night. He kissed her as if they had all the time in the world. As the tip of his tongue traced over her lips, her nipples grew hard, begging to be touched. What did it even mean? Why would he touch them? It didn't matter, they needed to be touched. She pressed herself wantonly against his chest, just as his tongue slipped into her mouth. Pleasure pulsed through her body, forcing a moan from her throat.

Ash pulled back, his own breathing labored. "Are you alright?"

"Yes, but I don't understand these feelings." She felt like such a fool. Were these feelings normal? She'd certainly never experienced anything like this with Greg. Her cheeks warmed with what she was about to say, but she trusted Ash not to judge her. "I want something, desperately, but I don't really even know what it is."

Ash's brow furrowed. "Have you never experienced sexual pleasure, Gwen?"

"I don't know." She shrugged and lowered her gaze, humiliated at her lack of knowledge after having been as good as married for a year.

Ash lifted her chin. "Don't be embarrassed, Gwen. You would know if you had, and if you haven't, that certainly isn't your fault."

She shrugged again. "I guess I haven't then."

"Would you like me to show you?"

Her mouth went dry. "Do you mean—" She felt like a nitwit, struggling to even say the words out loud. "Do you mean the marriage act?"

"No." He shook his head. "I would keep my clothes on, just as they are, and we wouldn't even need to move from this chair. That something your body is longing for? I can give you that."

A delicious shudder rushed through her body at his words and she nodded eagerly.

"You have to promise me something, though. If at any point you want me to stop, you'll tell me."

"I won't want you to stop."

"You don't know that. Promise me, Gwen. If at any moment you want me to stop, even if it's just for a second, just say the word hairpin. I will stop without the slightest hesitation."

"Hairpin?" She giggled.

"I know it sounds silly, but it's important."

"Very well. I promise. Now can we get on with it?"

His laugh was deep and rich and it warmed her to her very soul.

———

Ash couldn't quite believe he was doing this. It was reckless and he knew it. He had those rules in place for a reason, but when she'd said she didn't want to marry again, what she'd meant was she won't get a chance to experience these things. Not that she'd ever had a chance. How many times had the bastard taken her in his pursuit of a child, and hadn't once shown her pleasure? The more Ash learned about that piece of filth, the more he vowed that he would kill him. He wasn't going to let him ruin this night, though, so he put the blackguard out of his mind.

He wrapped his arms around Gwen, pulling her into his embrace. Her lips were soft and eager as he slowly savored them. She was quickly learning. Her tongue flicked over his lips, drawing an unexpected moan from him. He felt her smile against his lips. Bringing her pleasure was going to be an exquisite form of self-flagellation, but he was determined to be the one to provide it for her.

She whimpered as he plunged his tongue into her mouth, pressing her breasts against his chest. Her hard nipples were seeking attention, and she probably didn't understand what they needed, but he did. Reaching a hand between them, he lifted her breast gently in his palm and she whimpered against his mouth. He flicked the tip of his tongue against hers and then repeated the motion with his thumb across her excited nipple.

She gasped, pulling her mouth from his, her eyes wide with wonder.

"Do you want me to stop?" he asked.

"No," she said breathlessly. "I want more."

Oh, she would have more. Right now, Ash would give her the moon and the stars if she asked for them. She stared intently at his hand as he strummed her nipple again, earning him another grateful moan.

There was too much fabric between them. He reached down and placed his hand on the sash at her waist. "May I?"

She didn't speak, but simply untied it herself and threw the wrapper open, leaving only the thin fabric of her nightgown. Ash chuckled. How had this passionate, incredible woman never experienced pleasure? It wasn't right.

He locked his gaze with hers as he lowered his head and flicked his tongue across her nipple. Gwen sucked in a breath but didn't divert her wondering gaze. She watched, enthralled as he lapped at her nipple again and again, soaking the fabric of her nightgown. As he repeated the ritual with the other nipple, her fingers slid into his hair. With each flick of his tongue, her grip tightened and her body twitched in response.

"Ash!" Her voice was breathless as she wiggled in his lap, desperate for relief. His own desire was painful, but finding his own release was not part of what was happening with Gwen tonight.

He had planned to draw this out and make it a bit more of a seduction, but he could tell she was already fairly close and so far, he'd only teased her nipples. She was incredibly responsive to his touch. He brushed his hand down her belly and pressed his fingers lightly at the juncture of her thighs. "Is this where you want me to touch you?"

She swallowed, her eyes filled mostly with desire, but a touch of uncertainty, as well. She nodded. "Yes. Is that normal, Ash?"

"It's normal, and it's wonderful." He kissed her thoroughly, trying to fan the flames of her desire and put her concerns at ease.

"I can do it through your nightgown, if that's more

comfortable for you, but the pleasure will be more intense if my fingers are against your flesh without the fabric barrier. How would you like me to do it?"

She drew her bottom lip between her teeth, obviously conflicted about her answer.

"How about this?" He nipped softly at her lips. "We'll start on top of the nightgown and then if you're comfortable, and decide you want more, I'll give you more."

She nodded enthusiastically, but her thighs were still pressed tightly together. He traced his tongue up the side of her neck and whispered into her ear. "If you want to be touched, you'll have to open up, Gwen."

Her knees instantly parted for him and he dipped his fingers between her legs, swirling gently against her sensitive flesh. Even through the fabric of her nightgown, he could tell she was slick with need. The knowledge nearly sent him over the edge.

"My God, you're incredible, Gwen."

She groaned as he flicked his tongue over her nipple again, her hips bucking against his hand. "Oh—" She pushed herself more firmly against his fingers.

"Do you want me under the nightgown?"

She hesitated for a moment. "I do, but I think it's, I think I'm—"

"Wet?" he supplied. Her blush told him he'd guessed right. "God I hope you are," he growled, tugging up her gown and plunging his hand beneath.

He forced himself to slow down. To master himself

and control his own lust. The last thing he wanted to do was frighten her. He took a breath and lightly rested his fingers against her hot flesh. Wet was not generous enough a word for what she was. He gently slid two fingers into her folds, caressing her sensitive nub between them.

She called out, her legs jerking with the pleasure. As he circled with his fingers, his tongue copied the movements inside her mouth. He longed to feel his fingers inside of her, to have the walls of her body surrounding him, but he didn't want to do anything that might remind her of her past. Instead, he focused every fiber of his being on her and stoking her growing pleasure.

Slow and steady, he continued with his rhythm, stroking her as her body quivered, her moans growing louder and more urgent with each caress.

"That's it," he encouraged.

Her eyes grew wide as she neared her climax. "Ash, I don't know."

"It's alright, Gwen. I've got you. Just let go and enjoy."

And at those words, she took her pleasure. "Ash!" she called out, throwing her head back. He groaned his own pleasure at the sound of his name being shouted from her lips in ecstasy. She writhed in his arms, as glorious as a goddess. Her breasts heaved as she cried out with each wave of pleasure as it crashed through her.

As she calmed, he pulled her nightgown back down

and gathered her against his chest. That was the most incredible thing he'd ever experienced. How was that even possible when he was still as hard as a steel rod with no relief in sight? Her panting breaths whispered across his neck as he rubbed a hand over her shoulder. He pressed a kiss against the top of her head.

"I don't really think it's sufficient," Gwen said quietly against his neck, "but, thank you."

Ash squeezed her in a tight embrace. "I assure you, it was my pleasure."

He waited for the guilt and self-loathing to come, but they didn't. Somehow it just felt right with Gwen. She wasn't giving herself to him out of fear or to gain his favor. But was that really true? Or was he just trying to justify what he'd done with her?

"Please don't send me away tonight."

How could he possibly refuse such a sweet request? Besides, holding her in his arms was the only thing that had kept his nightmares at bay, and even though he really shouldn't, he would gladly allow her to do that again.

"I wouldn't dream of it, my angel."

CHAPTER NINE

When Gwen woke the following morning, he was still there beside her. His warmth and his spicy scent wrapped around her like a comforting embrace. She shamelessly threw an arm and a leg over him and snuggled herself against him.

"Mmmm. Don't make me wake up," she mumbled. "I'm enjoying this."

His chest shook with a soft chuckle, but he just rubbed her shoulder. Eventually, she opened her eyes and smiled up at him.

"You're still here."

"And I'm glad I am. Otherwise, I would have missed that lovely smile." He rewarded her with an affectionate smile of his own. Her heart stumbled a bit, warnings flashing in her brain. She knew she was setting herself up for heartbreak with Ash, but these moments would make it all worth it. Or at least, that's what she told herself. She'd have these times to look back on forever, once he was gone. And he would be gone, at least emotionally. Once they returned to Raven House, he would put his walls back up and separate himself from her. He'd have to. But for now, she had him here, in her arms, and in her heart.

"We need to talk, and if we do it here in my bed, no one would dare to interrupt us."

"Well, that sounds ominous. Should I be worried?"

He gave her a gentle squeeze. "Nothing to worry about. I just want to tell you some things before you hear them from someone else."

She nodded, trepidation settling in her stomach, despite his assurances.

"Warwick is going to be arrested today."

"For what he did to that maid?"

"No, unfortunately, the only punishment he'll get for that is the black eye and broken ribs I provided yesterday."

"Well, I'm glad to hear he's at least in some pain."

Ash chuckled. "I didn't have you down as someone who enjoys violence."

"That poor girl will never be the same because of him. So if that's not the reason he's being arrested, then why?"

A brief shadow passed over his face before he

answered. "He's been providing fake marriages for people."

Gwen gasped, pressing a hand over her mouth. Bile tried to make its way up her throat. She swallowed, forcing it down along with the anguish that flooded through her.

"Do you mean my marriage?"

His eyes held the answer as they filled with sorrow, but he nodded anyway.

"I knew he was somehow familiar, but I still just can't place where I could have seen him. It's like he's just not quite right."

"It was probably his brother you're remembering. I haven't seen the man, but presumably they share some resemblance. He's an actual vicar and is the one who has been performing these sham weddings."

He was right. It was the vicar. She hadn't really paid that much attention to him at the time, she'd been fixated on Greg, but now she could remember him. Fear and anger knotted inside her belly. "Do you mean there are others like me?"

"I'm afraid so."

She was scared to ask, but she needed to know. "How many others?"

"We don't know yet, but this has been going on for years, so it won't be only a few."

Tears ran, unbidden, from her eyes. She wasn't entirely sure why she was crying. Was it pain knowing that other women had been through what she had? Or relief that she wasn't alone?

"I'm so sorry, Gwen. If I had been here to take care of my responsibilities rather than running off to build my ridiculous raven empire, perhaps I could have prevented all of it." He rolled so he could wrap both of his arms around her.

After a moment, she slowly pushed him back so she could look into his eyes. "If you had been here, Ash, who would have rescued me from the streets in the first place? What other man would have allowed me to pick his pockets, and then rather than seeing me punished for the deed, given me warmth, food, shelter, and a soft place to lay my head?"

He closed his eyes for a moment before a small, tentative smile grew on his lips. "You were the cutest little pickpocket, though."

Gwen pressed herself back into his embrace. Life had been so difficult before she'd met him that day. When her father died, all he'd left her with was debt. She'd quickly found herself on the streets, and somehow, she'd been successful enough at picking pockets that she'd never had to resort to selling her body. And then, that day, she'd seen Ash. Immaculately pressed and groomed, dressed in his usual black from head to toe, sunlight gleaming off his perfectly shined shoes. His raven topped cane swung as he walked and a ring adorned his little finger. On that particular day, she'd had no idea who he was, but she'd seen him look at an expensive watch, and slip it into his pocket. That was what she was going to take, and she had thought she'd succeeded, until he'd whirled around and snatched her wrist.

"That ridiculous raven empire saved my life. It is your legacy, Ash. I know this is your title and your lineage, but it isn't all that you are. The good you've done in Raven Row, the lost souls you've saved and the women you've lifted up and given an opportunity for a better life, that will live on even long after you've gone."

Ash pressed a lingering kiss against her forehead. "Thank you, Gwen. That may be the kindest thing anyone has ever said to me."

It broke her heart that he couldn't see what a good man he was. Although, perhaps that's why he was so good. She obviously wasn't going to convince him, no matter how hard she tried, so she steered the conversation back to where it had begun.

"Will others be arrested for this marriage scheme, as well? I guess what I'm really asking is, will Greg be arrested?"

"Not if I get to him first." His voice was hard and as cold as ice. There were moments she'd glimpsed this side of him. The side that everyone in Raven Row seemed to know was there, but few had ever actually seen. If you had an ounce of sense, you didn't cross Ash, and you certainly didn't harm someone who was under his protection.

"Will you really kill him?" She spoke softly, a nervousness filling her belly.

"Without a moment's hesitation."

Gwen swallowed. "What if I don't want you to?"

Ash leaned back, his eyes scouring her face. "I know you cared for him, Gwen, but he's been nothing but an abuser to you. He led you straight into hell with his lies. If he had succeeded in getting you pregnant, what do you think would have happened after the baby was born?"

"I don't know." She'd never taken a moment to think about that. Until just a couple of days ago, he was her husband as far as she'd been concerned.

Ash's expression clouded with anger. "He would have stolen your child and abandoned you."

Nausea roiled in her stomach. How could she have been so naive? How could she have fallen for his false-hoods and his fake charm?

Ash's warm hand brushed soothingly along her arm. "I will see that he's punished for all the pain he caused you, Gwen. I promise."

"But he's not the reason I don't want you to kill him, Ash. It's you."

His brows lowered in confusion. "You don't need to worry, Gwen. He won't hurt me. I've handled worse than him."

"But what of your soul?"

His answering laughter was filled with cynicism. "My soul is long past hope of redemption."

"Don't say that."

He ignored her plea and instead pressed another kiss against her forehead. "I need to get up and face the day, but you are welcome to laze around in my bed for a while longer if you'd like."

"Do you have to leave right away again?"

"I have a few things to take care of, but I won't be away all day today."

"Is there any chance there's a library in this house? A book would really help with the boredom."

"There most certainly is, and a grand one at that."

"Do you mind if I have a look around in there?"

"You're not a prisoner here, Gwen. You are free to do whatever you'd like."

———

Christ. Ash was in trouble. He sat at the desk in his study, staring down at paperwork but not really seeing it. All he could see was Gwen. He needed to finish up here and get back to Raven Row where everything could return to normal.

It wasn't even just Gwen, everything in his life seemed to be changing. He seemed to be changing.

Sleeping with Gwen in his arms and pleasuring her in his lap.

So much for his rules.

Showing his scars to Trent, a virtual stranger. No one ever saw his scars, aside from his valet. Even Patrick and Michael had only ever seen glimpses of them. But he hadn't wanted Trent to be under any illusions that their father might have been a good man. He needed to know the truth. And then there was Fogg. Ash still wasn't sure what he was going to do with him. He'd gone back to arrange Warwick's arrest, which was for the better. Ash needed to put some other things to rest before he could decide Fogg's fate. Benson had been taking excellent care of him, although he still looked a bit haunted every time he saw Ash's back. He just couldn't see Benson at Raven House, though. He belonged in a country estate.

Just then, Fogg appeared in the doorway of his study looking unusually trepidatious.

"They're here to take Warwick."

Ash nodded, and slid the paperwork he was looking at into the right hand drawer. He followed Fogg from the room.

"Do they know about Gwen?"

Fogg shook his head. "I removed her name, and his, from the list I gave them. I assumed you'd want to deal with him yourself and that you wouldn't want Gwen's name dragged into this mess."

Ash nodded. "Thank you." This was why he didn't

know what to do with Fogg. He'd never been anything but loyal. If any other servant had laid hands on him, they'd have been gone, immediately, but Fogg was more than just his valet.

Ash greeted the officers and then watched in disgust as they escorted Warwick through the entrance hall. He was still going on about how he hadn't done anything and that maid was a whore, until they explained that he was actually being arrested for facilitating fraudulent marriages. His eyes bulged at the words and he finally went quiet as they led him out the front door.

One man stayed behind and came to stand beside Fogg.

"My lord, this is Simon Allister, the man who's been leading the investigation into Warwick and his associates."

"It's a pleasure to meet you, my lord. I am in your debt for helping to bring this all together and for detaining the main perpetrator so that we could simply come and collect him."

"It's unfortunate that Fogg wouldn't allow me to just kill the blackguard."

Allister chuckled. "Don't worry. We'll be sure he gets what he deserves."

"What kind of punishment is he looking at?"

Allister shrugged. "The church, and therefore the crown, takes this sort of thing very seriously. Suffice it to say, he won't be a problem again."

Ash nodded. "Glad to hear it."

"Before I go, my lord, I was hoping that, sometime in the near future, you and I could have a conversation. The intelligence services have a proposition for you."

Ash raised a skeptical brow. "Somehow I doubt that the intelligence services really want help from someone like me. Besides, I will be returning to my club in London, as soon as possible."

"The proposition involves your club, my lord."

What was this? Ash didn't like surprises, especially ones that felt a bit suspicious. "Well then, you know where to find me when I'm back in London."

"Thank you, my lord." He bowed before turning and nodding at Ash's valet. "Fogg."

The man left, but Fogg didn't follow. "Are you not going with him?" Ash asked.

Fogg hesitated before answering. "I wasn't planning on it." He inhaled a nervous breath. Nervous was not something Fogg often seemed to be. "Can we talk, Ash?"

"I suppose we ought to," Ash said gruffly. He turned and stalked back toward his study. This was a necessary conversation, but one Ash wasn't sure he was ready for yet.

He sat down behind his desk while Fogg closed the door.

"I know you're angry with me, Ash."

"I'm not angry with you, Fogg." He paused for a moment. "Alright, that's not true. I am bloody furious.

But I'm also conflicted, and I don't know what to do with you."

"I know it doesn't change what I did, but I am sorry. I made a mistake, Ash. An inexcusable mistake."

"A day and a half you were gone, and when you return, you're suddenly questioning my judgment and putting your hands on me?" He stared directly into the man's eyes. "What am I supposed to do with that, Fogg?"

Fogg wrapped his arms around his stomach, as if physically protecting himself would also protect him from his emotions. For anyone else, Fogg was difficult to read, but Ash's livelihood depended on reading people, and he'd known Fogg a long time. Right now, the man was genuinely remorseful, and uncharacteristically scared.

"My actions were unacceptable, but my heart was in the right place, Ash."

"I know that. You wouldn't be sitting here otherwise. But your job has never been, and will never be, to protect me from my own actions."

"I understand. I also understand if you have to let me go, but I can promise, if you do keep me on, I'll never do something like that again."

"Damnit, Fogg!" Ash slammed his palm against the top of the desk and the man jumped. "Why did you put me in this position?"

"I'm sorry, Ash."

It was obvious he was, but that didn't make it any easier.

"Is it truly a one-off? Or have you just gotten too big for your britches? Because you sure were comfortable slamming me, bodily, into a chair."

"Perhaps I did become a bit full of myself, but it was a momentary lapse, and I won't let it happen again."

Ash let out a long sigh. Fogg had clearly been humbled by this experience, which was good. He really didn't want to lose him. Despite his actions, Ash didn't question his loyalty.

"See that it doesn't," he said quietly.

Fogg nodded, but it took a moment for the meaning of the words to sink in. His eyes flicked to Ash's face, his breathing accelerating. "Does that... does that mean I can stay?"

"Yes."

Fogg exhaled a huff of relief. "Thank you, Ash. I promise I won't make you regret it."

Ash nodded once. "Let's not talk any more about it. It's in the past now."

"Thank you."

"So what happened to the footman I left you with?"

"I let him go back to work. I assume you scared him straight."

"Me? You're the one who threatened to cut out his tongue and send it to his mother."

Fogg chuckled. "I did, didn't I?" He shrugged. "I

wanted to be sure he wouldn't tell anyone what I'd just done to you."

"I think you accomplished that. I suppose I should probably talk to the poor young man and assure him he's not going to meet a violent end. He's probably scared half to death working here now."

Fogg shrugged. "Perhaps, but I bet he'll never steal from you again."

Ash shook his head. He preferred his employees to not be terrified of him. "Now, what have you managed to discover about the man who took advantage of Gwen?"

"Well, we know the address where he was living from the letters, but he seems to have run off and gone into hiding. I have assigned someone to watch the house, as well as his townhouse in London. He's going to be a little bit tricky to... see to."

Ash raised a brow. "Why is that?"

"He's the third son of a very wealthy baron. Which seems to be the reason for this whole charade. Apparently, in order to inherit anything, he has to produce at least one son. He's been married for five years with no offspring."

"It seems like a lot of effort to procure a child. There are plenty of desperate women, pregnant out of wedlock and happy to sell their baby."

Fogg shrugged. "Perhaps he was set on it being from his own loins?"

"Or perhaps he saw an opportunity to live out some depraved fantasy."

"I don't know any of the details of what occurred with Gwen while he had her."

"She has marks on her body, and he's been forcing himself on her for a year in an attempt to get her pregnant."

A shadow settled over Fogg's eyes and a muscle ticked beside his eye. He loathed mistreatment of women as much as Ash. They were kindred spirits in that regard.

"We'll find him, Ash, and baron's son or not, we'll deal with him."

"I"—Ash pointed to his chest—"will personally see to him. Make sure everyone knows that. He needs to still be alive and conscious when I meet him. I want to see the fear and pain on his face as I inflict it." A shiver raced through Ash's body as rage washed over him.

"Understood."

There was a knock at the door. "Come," Ash called.

Moulton opened the door. "My lord, you have a visitor. A Mr. Gibson. I've put him and the child in the blue drawing room."

The announcement raised his spirits immensely. "Excellent, Moulton. I'll be down shortly. Please see that they have tea and some scones or something to eat."

"Yes, my lord." He bowed and was gone.

Fogg's brow was raised, but he didn't say a word.

"Don't you dare to start walking on eggshells, Fogg."

He chuckled. "Very well. Who the devil is here to see you? And with a child?"

"That's more like it." Ash shrugged. "Turns out I have a half-brother."

"When were you going to tell me about that?"

"When you decided to stop being a prat."

Fogg choked on a laugh. "Touché."

CHAPTER
TEN

It took Gwen a bit of wandering before she eventually found the library. Ash hadn't exaggerated when he'd said it was grand. As she skimmed her hand over the spines of countless books, her mind seemed unable to focus enough to see what any of them even were. There were so many thoughts tumbling about in there. She could still see Ash's hand disappearing under her nightgown and his tongue flicking her nipple through wet cotton fabric. Even now, the thoughts made warmth settle in her belly. How was it possible that his touch could make her feel so incredible?

He was so gentle and so kind and caring. It made it difficult to imagine him being violent with anyone, but he'd talked of killing Greg as if it were nothing. He said he'd dealt with worse than him, so he'd presumably killed before. It was such a conundrum, such a strange juxtaposition to have in one person. But perhaps it all actually came from the same place, a fierce need to keep those around him safe and protected. He certainly wasn't prone to brutality or violent outbursts. He would never hurt any of the women in his care. He didn't even raise his voice around them.

Her mind conjured his smile. There'd been so much compassion as he'd shown her that incredible pleasure. He'd been tender and gentle, his eyes constantly checking to make sure she was comfortable. She let out a long sigh. Her heart was in serious trouble. And yet, she knew without a doubt that she would go to him again tonight.

She forced herself to focus on the titles of the books before her and eventually saw one she recognized, Jane Eyre. She'd never actually read it, but she'd heard of it. She pulled it off the shelf and slowly made her way from the library. Her mind was still swirling, and it was unlikely she'd be able to concentrate enough to actually read, but she had to try.

When she reached the end of the wide corridor, where it led into the entrance hall, Ash was coming down the stairs. He leaned on his cane but had a smile on his lips that took her breath away. She stopped and just watched him.

———

Ash had barely made it to the bottom of the stairs when Maggie came running across the entrance hall toward him. "Uncle Ash!" she called, her curls bouncing, a smile beaming on her face.

He crouched down to greet her and she held up a doll. "Look what I got!"

"A doll? You lucky girl!"

She nodded animatedly and pointed at her own chest. "And I got this dress that's the same as hers!"

"Wow! You must have been an awfully good girl to deserve something so special."

"I was!" She hugged the doll to her chest and moved closer, holding out her free arm.

Ash didn't have much experience with young children, but presumably that meant she wanted him to pick her up. He lifted her into his arms before settling one of them under her bottom. Only then did he see Gwen looking on from the hallway that led to the library. Ash smiled sheepishly at her and shrugged.

Trent stood in the drawing room doorway. "I'm sorry. She was too excited to wait for you."

"Can you blame her? Her brother bought her a new dress, and a doll with a matching one."

His lips turned up in a grateful smile. Ash summoned Gwen with a tilt of his head. She followed them into the room. He set Maggie back on her feet and moved to the tea tray. "Are you hungry, Poppet? There are some delicious looking cakes here." He leaned down and spoke softly. "The lemon seed ones are my favorite."

"Mine too!" She snatched one from the plate and took a bite. "Mmmm."

He stood to make introductions. "Gwen, this is Trent, my half-brother." Gwen did a good job of hiding her shock at the news, but he could tell she was bursting with questions. "Trent, this is Gwen, my employee."

Ash saw a hint of guilt settle on Trent's features. He was remembering his disparaging words from the night before, which was exactly what Ash had hoped for. He wanted Trent to see that the women who worked for him were respectable and deserved to be treated as such.

"It's a pleasure to meet you, Gwen."

"Likewise," Gwen replied.

"And this beautiful young lady is Maggie." Maggie skipped over, her mouth full with another bite of cake.

Gwen crouched beside her. "That sure is a lovely dress."

Maggie shimmied to make the fabric sway, a giggle bubbling up in her joy. How could her happiness bring him so much warmth? He couldn't have any actual nieces or nephews, and he certainly didn't plan to have any children of his own, but this little girl was already so precious to him.

"Maggie," Ash said, getting the girl's attention. "Your brother and I have some business to take care of. How would you feel about going up to the nursery with Gwen to see what toys you can find there? Surely there must be something up there you'd enjoy playing with." Her eyes grew wide and she nodded.

Ash moved to ring for Mrs. Archer, but then saw a whole group of servants gathered in the hall, his housekeeper among them. He couldn't blame them for wanting to get a glimpse of his guest. Anyone with a pair of eyes would guess they were brothers, which would only heighten their curiosity. "Mrs. Archer?"

She hurried across the hall to the drawing room. "Yes, my lord?"

"Will you please show Gwen and Maggie up to the nursery? I know it's been closed up for a very long time, but just do the best you can." He lowered his voice so only she would hear. "And get everyone back to work. I don't need onlookers or eavesdroppers."

"Yes, my lord. Of course." She turned and glared at the other servants and they immediately dispersed.

Ash grabbed the tray of food and handed it to the housekeeper. "Take this with you so she can nibble on them if she decides to."

Gwen took Maggie's hand. Ash leaned down and whispered into her ear on her way out of the room. "I promise I'll explain everything later. Thank you for showing me so much grace."

"I look forward to hearing the story this evening, my lord." The little minx winked at him before turning and leaving the room.

Feeling a bit discomfited, Ash sighed and turned back to Trent. "Why don't we go up to my study? We're less likely to have an audience up there."

Trent's gaze traveled over every detail as they moved through the house, clearly not accustomed to so much extravagance. Who would be, really?

"Have a seat," Ash said as they entered his study. He closed the door as Trent settled himself in front of his desk. Ash poured two glasses of brandy and set one in front of Trent before sitting across from him.

Trent picked up the glass, examining its contents before setting it back down. His dark eyes wandered aimlessly about the room looking slightly bewildered.

"I don't really know how to do this."

"How to drink brandy?" Ash teased.

Trent's laugh sounded subdued, and he looked a little overwhelmed. "I mean, all of this." He waved his hand aimlessly. "The luxury, the house, the servants, the crystal and expensive spirits, and especially you." His eyes came up to meet Ash's. "Particularly in this grand house, I don't feel right not addressing you by your title. And all of the kindness you've shown me and Maggie and—"

"Trent," Ash said, cutting him off. "I don't know how to do this either, but we'll just figure it out, won't we?"

Trent nodded.

"I promise I didn't put poison in that brandy."

Trent smiled meekly and took a sip. He nodded appreciatively.

"I need to apologize about something from last night, Ash."

"You don't need to apologize about anything, Trent."

"I do," he said more firmly. "I should not have used that word when I mentioned the women who work for you. It was disrespectful to them, and I regretted it the moment it left my mouth. I don't use words like that, and I'm sorry."

Ash raised his glass. "Thank you." The truth was, he was actually very pleased that Trent insisted on apologizing for that. It spoke to how he felt toward women.

"Feel free to tell me if I'm being impertinent, but is Gwen one of the women who works in your club?"

"She was, and she will be again. Unfortunately, she was one of the women involved in the fake marriage scheme. Luckily, fate somehow brought her to my doorstep, once more."

"My God. I wish I'd known that was happening. Perhaps I could have done something." He shook his head dejectedly.

"What's done is done. As horrible as it is, there is no undoing any of it now. We can only hope the people involved are punished sufficiently."

"I suppose you're right."

"Now," Ash said. "I have done a lot of thinking since I

met you last night, and I want to see that you're taken care of."

"Ash, you don't owe me anything."

He held up a hand to stop him. "I know I don't, but let me finish. I believe I have a solution that will benefit us both."

Trent nodded. "I'm listening."

"I have no family. My parents and my brother are all dead." Ash sipped his brandy. "I don't want to just dismiss the fact that I suddenly have a brother, and a niece." The muscles in Trent's jaw were tight and he folded his arms across his chest. This was difficult for him. Ash knew what it was to not want to accept help or kindness from people.

"Let me tell you how I'd like it to go, and then you can tell me your opinions. First up, I'd like to settle some money on you, that should have been rightfully yours when our father died."

Trent shook his head. "I don't want charity from you, Ash."

"It's not charity. Like I said, it should have been rightfully yours. In addition to that, I'm in need of an estate manager. I know you're not trained for that, but I also know you've been watching the comings and goings on this estate for a year. It's clear that you're smart and resourceful, and you even have a family connection to the estate. Is that something you'd be interested in learning if I brought someone in to teach you?"

"How could you possibly trust me to manage your estate? You don't even know me, and the small amount you do know isn't good."

"I'm a fairly good judge of character. Besides that, I won't be making the same mistakes I made before. There will be a lot of eyes around here, and everyone will have access to me. I'm leaving, but I won't be disconnecting the same way I did before. I won't be just abandoning this place. So I'm going to make the choice to trust you, and I hope that in time, you'll prove me right. Until then, there will be checks and balances in place to ensure everyone is taken care of. It is a big job, though, so you certainly don't have to take it on."

"I would be honored to, and will do my best to learn as much and as quickly as I can."

"Good man!" Ash wasn't sure if he'd actually agree to it, and was truly pleased he had.

"And for what it's worth, I would be grateful to have you as my brother, Ash."

These sensations of warmth in his heart were still so foreign to him, but they'd happened several times these past few days. From Gwen and Benson, Maggie, and now Trent. Is this what it felt like to have a family who cared about one another?

Ash raised his glass. "To our future, whatever it may hold."

"To our future." Trent clinked his glass against Ash's and they both downed the remainder of their brandy.

"I'll reach out to Lord and Lady Epworth. I know them personally, and their estate isn't far from here. He'll be helpful for knowing who to bring in to train you up, and they have young children, so Lady Epworth will know where to start in finding a governess for Maggie."

Trent held up his hands. "Whoa. I feel like you and I have very different visions of this, Ash. Surely, an estate manager does not earn enough to afford a governess, not to mention, there's not an extra room in the home I'm living in."

"I just assumed you would live here."

"You what? Here?" He looked around the room again.

"I know this house is a lot, and it will take some getting used to, but it would be beneficial for us both. You'd be here to oversee everything. And it's a massive house. It seems silly for it to just sit empty while you're living in barely more than a shack."

"I've worked hard to be able to afford that shack."

"I know you have, and I'm not discounting that. I'm in no way implying that you can't make it on your own without my money. You obviously can. You've done just fine, and you've worked hard to provide for yourself and Maggie. You'll work hard here, too, Trent. And I know you want the best for Maggie. I believe living here and being provided with a good education will give her a leg up in life. It will give her opportunities that, I'm sorry to say, she wouldn't be afforded without those things."

Trent nodded, but he wasn't happy. He let out a long sigh. "It still feels like charity to me."

"And yet, I feel as if I'm taking advantage of you. I'm asking you to take on immense responsibilities that should really be mine. The truth is, I can never live here. There are simply too many nightmares from my past that still reside within these walls. I found my brother's lifeless body hanging in his room. I looked on as my mother was beaten to death in hers. I endured countless beatings, many of them in this very room. I can't get away from those things here, which is why I left in the first place, and why I must leave again."

"It's so hard to believe that such horrific things happened in a place filled with so much beauty and lavishness. Enduring all of that, how in God's name did you end up a decent man? Why are you not the despot that he was?"

Ash shrugged. "There, but for the grace of God, go I."

Trent shook his head. "No. I don't believe that. You're a good man. You're not simply masquerading as one."

"Hopefully you're right. Now, I would like to leave here and get back to my normal life, as soon as possible. I would feel better about leaving if I knew there was someone here I could trust, and for whatever reason, I believe I can trust you."

"You can."

Ash nodded. "Good. Let's get you moved in, then. You and Maggie can choose your bedrooms today."

Trent closed his eyes and inhaled deeply. "This feels like a dream, like it can't possibly be real."

Ash got to his feet and came around the desk. "You'll feel differently once you've taken on the workload." Trent stood and the two of them embraced, thumping each other on the back. He had a brother. In truth, it felt a bit like a dream to him, too. "I'll show you around, and then we'll collect Maggie from the nursery."

———

Gwen groaned with bliss as she lowered herself into the hot bathwater. She would miss this tub when they left this place. Perhaps she could convince Ash that he should get some like this for Raven House.

Ash was definitely putting things into place quickly for their departure. Not that she could blame him. She didn't know what all had happened in this house, but she knew that he had nightmares here. Nightmares that terrified him enough that he had allowed her to sleep in his bed again last night to avoid them. His rules were rigid, and he never broke them, so it spoke to the horror of what awaited him in his sleep.

But tonight, they had dined with Trent and Maggie. She was a delightful little girl and Ash simply doted on her. He'd laughed and smiled and teased. Gwen's heart warmed remembering the scene. He would be a wonderful father if he ever had children. Although, he'd never talked of settling down or finding a wife. He'd certainly never said anything about producing an heir. The truth was, that was none of her business.

Soon, they would be back in Raven Row and things would go back to how they had been once before. He, the illustrious, if kind, club owner, and she his employee. He treated all of the Lady Ravens as one might a sister. She sighed as she rubbed the washcloth over her shoulder. She didn't want things to go back to the way they had been before. Not that she wasn't grateful for what he would provide for her. Of course she was. Who knows what would have happened to her if he hadn't appeared at that cabin on the very night she had taken refuge there. It wouldn't have been good, that was assuredly true. For saving her from a horrible fate, she would be eternally grateful, but she would still wish it could be like this with him forever. She'd simply have to enjoy whatever time she could with him, for as long as it lasted. Perhaps tonight, she could convince him to give her more of that exquisite pleasure he'd introduced her to.

After Mary finished plaiting her hair, she excused her for the night. Feeling very wicked, she removed her nightgown and wrapped herself in nothing but her robe. Perhaps it was a bit immodest, but if Ash was to repeat what he'd done last night, it would provide easier access for his magical fingers. Her stomach fluttered just thinking about it.

She tied the sash at her waist and slid her feet into

her slippers. Excitement brewing within her, she made the now familiar walk through his dressing room and listened at the door to his bedroom. All was quiet. Slowly, she opened the door and peered inside. A fire burned in the grate, but Ash wasn't there. Not in the chair or in the bed. Perhaps she would wait for him by the fire.

She sat for an hour, but he never appeared. He was probably avoiding her again. She couldn't accept that. The time she had with him here was limited. He couldn't be ending it already. She wasn't ready to let him go.

She left his room and set out in search of him. Before she got far, the resonant sounds of piano music filled the air. All she had to do was follow them to their source, and there he was. His back was to her as she entered the dimly lit ballroom, his broad shoulders flexing as he moved with the unfamiliar melody. He'd dispensed with his coat and waistcoat and his black sleeves were rolled to just below his elbows. His body moved lithely as the music poured out of his soul through his fingers. No wonder his fingers had been so good at bringing her pleasure. Her cheeks warmed at the thought.

Moving slowly, careful not to make a sound, she made her way closer. The notes crescendoed, forcing her to draw in a breath and goosebumps to rise on her skin, and then they slowed, the volume ebbing. The music lulled her into such a beautiful calm before it trailed to an end.

"Good evening, Gwen." He picked up the glass of brandy from on top of the piano and took a sip.

"Don't stop on my account. I was very much enjoying that."

He patted the bench beside him, and a thrill rushed through her. She'd thought for certain he was going to tell her to go to bed. The chill of the bench quickly penetrated her robe to her skin beneath, reminding her just how little she was wearing.

Ash turned to look at her, his gaze dipping to the front of her robe. He closed his eyes and whispered, "Lord, give me strength."

She felt a blush creep up her cheeks. "How did you know I was here? I didn't make a sound."

His eyes slid open, hunger darkening their already rich depths. "Your tantalizing aroma filled the air as soon as you entered."

"Mary did put rose in my bathwater."

"I'd ask what you're doing here, Gwen, but your choice of attire makes that fairly obvious."

"I waited for you in your bedchamber, but you never came."

He rubbed a hand roughly across his forehead. Turning toward her, he took hold of one of her hands. "We have to stop this, Gwen. Tonight is our last night here. Tomorrow we leave for Raven House."

The words cleaved her heart in two. She wasn't ready

for this to end. She certainly wasn't going to give up this one last night with him.

"But that's all the more reason you shouldn't send me away tonight."

CHAPTER
ELEVEN

"You really do make it impossible for me to say no."

Gwen hesitated for a moment, uncertainty settling over her. "Am I pressuring you to do things you don't want to do, Ash? That wasn't my intention."

He huffed a laugh and rolled his eyes. "Quite the opposite, Gwen. I want these things with you more than you can possibly imagine, but I also know I shouldn't. As your employer it isn't right for me to take liberties."

"Well, we're in luck, then, because tonight, here in this house, you're not my employer. You're just a man." She rubbed a hand over his shoulder and down his arm. "A handsome, strong, kind, intelligent, wonderful man, who I adore." She cupped his cheek in her palm. His gaze was locked with hers and she watched as his throat worked with a swallow.

"I must be the luckiest man alive to have the privilege of having you in my life again."

"Or the unluckiest." She giggled. "All I've ever been for you is a headache, picking your pockets and breaking all your rules."

"Mmmm." He lifted her chin and pressed his soft lips against hers. "But you've also been my angel. The truth is, I was terrified of finally returning here. I knew the nightmares would haunt me again once I was within these walls. But then you arrived, brave and kind and unyielding, chasing them away. You've held them at bay these past nights, keeping me safe from my terrors, and I will be eternally grateful for that." He pressed a gentle kiss to her forehead.

"So, I suppose the least I can do on our last night here is see that you're thoroughly sated." A decadent vow flashed in his eyes and warmth pooled in her stomach as desire streaked through her. He got up from the bench and offered her a hand, but he didn't escort her from the room as she'd expected him to. Reclaiming her lips, he crushed her to him, his tongue sending rivers of desire racing through her as it plunged inside her mouth. She whimpered, overwhelmed with need as his hands roved over her back.

He wrapped them around her bottom, and surprised a squeak from her when he lifted her onto the piano. The shock of the cold surface through her robe, was quickly tempered by the heat that raged through her body. He took her mouth with a savage intensity, and she returned what he offered with reckless abandon. He stepped between her legs as she spread them wantonly. His strong hands gripped her hips and pulled her to the edge of the piano. Her robe had parted, leaving the fabric of his trousers as the only barrier separating the bulge within, and the sensitive flesh between her thighs. Was he going to take her? To press himself inside of her? Why did a part of her long for that with Ash? Long to be connected to him, to have his body inside hers?

He reached between them and untied the sash before pulling the fabric of her robe open. Holding her in place with his steadying hands on her thighs, he took a step back and allowed his gaze to sweep over her body. She'd never been so vulnerably naked before, her legs spread wide for his eyes to devour every inch of her. And they did. She wasn't embarrassed or ashamed because what she saw in his eyes as they scoured her, was sheer awe.

"My God, Gwen. You are staggeringly beautiful." His tongue flicked out to wet his lips and his breath was shaky.

She'd never thought of herself as beautiful. She had a rounded belly and thighs that were short and stout like the rest of her. But she didn't doubt his sincerity. His reaction left no doubt that he, at least, found her to be to his liking.

He groaned softly as his tongue seared along her collarbone, as if he'd been dying to taste her. His clear desire had wetness already pooling between her thighs, and he had hardly touched her yet. Goosebumps rose on her skin as his tongue glided up her neck and he nibbled gently on her earlobe.

His hand skimmed over her ribs before her breast was settled in his warm palm. She groaned, her needy nipple swelling against him, demanding his attention. It had felt good through her nightgown, but having her skin against his with no barrier was incredible. He nipped kisses down her throat as he gently massaged her breast.

"How do you make me feel so good?" she murmured as his mouth feathered kisses across her chest. His lips turned up with an evocative hum.

"I'm just getting started."

He swooped down and drew her other nipple into his fiery mouth. Sensations shot through her body and she nearly bucked herself right off of the piano. He wrapped an arm around her waist and pressed himself more firmly between her legs.

"Don't worry, I won't let you fall, Angel." The term of endearment sent a whole other kind of joy rushing through her. It made her feel special and cherished.

Pleasure careened through her with each flick of his tongue, until she was squirming and rocking herself shamelessly against his swollen manhood. He gripped her thighs firmly and took a step back, his eyes suddenly boring into hers.

"Don't you dare to find your own pleasure. That's my

job tonight." He plundered her mouth until she was breathless with need. Suddenly, his lips abandoned hers but they quickly wrapped themselves around her nipple. She gripped his hair, her body wriggling, desperately seeking out his touch. A powerful ache grew between her thighs.

Slowly, he laid her back onto the piano, his tongue searing a path between her breasts and down her stomach.

"Please, Ash." If he didn't touch her soon, surely she would burst with longing.

"As you wish, Angel." He pressed her thighs open wide and ducked his head. The tip of his tongue slid along her most sensitive flesh, from her entrance, all the way to the top of her sex.

Pleasure exploded and she slammed her hands against the hard surface of the piano, a loud crack echoing through the room. She braced herself, as if the paroxysm would somehow make her fall off. His resulting chuckle feathered over her delicate flesh. Never in her wildest dreams could she have imagined something so glorious. He lapped at her, sending bolts of pleasure through her body. She writhed and jerked as his expert touch pushed her to higher levels of ecstasy. Pleasure continued to build, throbbing through her body, making her legs shake and her hips buck wildly against his mouth.

His hands slid beneath her bottom, holding firmly to keep her still as he feasted.

"My God, you taste incredible." He lifted his head just long enough to utter the words before returning to his magical ministrations.

Hearing him speak of her that way made her heart race and sent her pleasure spiraling out of control.

She moaned his name.

His tongue continued in a rhythm that matched her pulse, driving the pleasurable sensations higher and higher. Desperate for release, she sank one hand into his hair, pulling him more tightly against her. The other hand tried to grip the smooth surface of the piano to steady herself. Just when she couldn't take any more, a cataclysm of pleasure erupted through her, transporting her to some kind of euphoric paradise.

She called out, incapable of words, only desperate sounds escaped her. Wave after wave of pleasure hurtled through her body. Ash didn't stop his sweet torture until her body finally began to calm.

"Mmmmm." His voice purred against her skin as he pressed soft kisses to her inner thigh. Slowly he stood and smiled down at her. He took one more long look at her body before he closed the sides of her robe and tied the sash at her waist. Stepping around to the side, he slid one arm under her knees and the other under her back, scooping her off of the piano.

Without a word, she wrapped her arms around his neck and rested her head against his shoulder as he carried her from the room and up the stairs. Her body was limp and languid, soft pulses of pleasure still flickering through her.

———

Climbing the stairs without his cane was painful, but Ash would happily endure it any time if it meant having Gwen's sated body in his arms. Nothing would ever compare to the wondrous experience of her coming undone on his piano while he devoured her luscious sex.

He carried her through the door to his bedroom and closed it with his hip. Lowering himself into one of the chairs, he settled her in his lap.

"Are you alright, Angel?"

She groaned softly. That must mean yes. After a few more minutes of silence, she sat up and let out a long sigh. She furrowed her brow and wiggled her bottom slightly. He was still achingly hard.

"I'm sorry, Gwen. Perhaps I shouldn't have put you on my lap in my current state."

She shook her head. "You don't have to spare my sensibilities, Ash. But what about you? What about your wants and your desires?"

"No," he said firmly. "We're not starting down that path."

She rolled her eyes. "Let me guess. It's against your rules."

"It most certainly is." His jaw clenched as she wiggled against him again.

"But what if I want you to take me?"

He simply shook his head. She didn't know what she was asking for.

"Why do you have to be such a good man, with all your many rules, Ash?"

"You don't understand, Gwen. If I was a good man, I wouldn't need all these rules."

She cupped her cool fingers around his cheek. "That's where you're wrong, Ash. You have the rules *because* you're a good man. If you weren't, they would be meaningless."

"I wish you were right, Gwen." His heart ached. More than anything, he wished he was the man she believed him to be.

"Then tell me why, Ash. You didn't have any trouble letting me believe that you've killed men." She turned in his lap to better face him.

"That's different, Gwen. Punishing men who have hurt people I care about does not make me a bully or an abuser."

"Then what does?"

He shook his head. Fear settled in his stomach at the thought of telling her. "Are you sure you really want to know? You will never see me the same way again."

She held his face in her hands, her gaze flicking back and forth between his eyes. "Yes. I'm sure."

He let out a long sigh. "Very well." Perhaps if she knew the truth, it would make it easier to end all of this. Perhaps she'd want nothing to do with him once she knew. He looked down, unable to meet her eyes as he confessed his horrific sins. "It started when I was thirteen years old. On my thirteenth birthday, actually." He fidgeted with the fabric of her robe, not sure if he could actually speak the words to her. He didn't want to see the shame that would inevitably appear on her face, but he suddenly had a burning need to tell her. For some reason, he wanted her to know all of him.

"What happened on your thirteenth birthday, Ash?"

A muscle ticked in his jaw as he remembered the scene. "My father, in this very room, as it happens." He swallowed over a lump in his throat. "Ordered a young housemaid to—" He cleared his throat. "Apologies, but I don't know how to make it any less lewd. He ordered her to pleasure me with her mouth."

He flicked a look up to her eyes, but they weren't filled with judgment. Instead, they held such kindness. "You were a child, Ash. Your father is the only one who did anything wrong. You were as much a victim that day, as the maid."

"Even if you were right, Gwen, that day was only the beginning." He looked up into her eyes then, willing her to see the monster that he truly was. "As I grew, I took advantage of more and more of them. I'd have them on their knees or over the back of a sofa or however else I pleased. I was a villain, no better than what I walked in on with Warwick. I abused those women relentlessly. Day after day after day." To his dismay, an agonized sob broke from his lips. Tears flooded down his cheeks, choking sobs crashing over him so powerfully, they rendered him nearly unable to draw breath. What was happening to him? He'd never cried a day in his wretched life.

Gwen wrapped her arms around his head, pulling him against her bosom. Her hand rubbed soothing caresses over his hair as he cried.

"No," he finally shouted. "No, I don't deserve your kindness." Irritably, he brushed the tears from his cheeks. "I caused those women untold damage. I was a savage that they must have loathed."

"Did you force yourself on them?"

"I didn't have to," he said angrily. "Just like I wouldn't have to with you."

"No," she said firmly, forcing him to look her in the eye. "This"—she gestured between them—"is not like that. What's happening between us is because I want it, not because you are in a position of power over me. Not because you're taking advantage of me. But we will come back to that later. First, we're going to talk about these other women. At the time that those encounters happened, did you know what you were doing was wrong or that you might be hurting them?"

The tears began to flow again as he shook his head. "But that doesn't excuse my behavior."

She held him to her again. "Of course it does, Ash. You were merely emulating what you'd seen. Doing what you thought was appropriate."

He leaned back. "Are you implying that because I didn't know any better, it somehow didn't hurt them?"

Her mouth turned up in a sad sort of smile. "You sweet, kind, wonderful, man. Those women were not victims of you, they were victims of your father. As were you."

"No. I don't get a pass just because my father was a beast."

Gwen raised her beautiful, pale brows. "From the moment you realized your behaviors might be hurtful, how many women have you done that with?"

"That's when I laid down rules for myself."

"So, how many?"

"It doesn't erase what I did, Gwen."

"How many?" she said sternly.

He let out a shaky breath. "Just you."

"And before me, when was the last time you were with a woman?"

"Why are we having this conversation, Gwen?" His voice was firm, but what he really felt was fear.

"How long, Ash?"

"Fourteen years. I don't see why that matters."

She closed her eyes. "You've been celibate for fourteen years because you're terrified of hurting someone. You've convinced yourself that you're a monster. This is your father's legacy, Ash. You can't allow it to devour your whole life."

"What would you suggest I do, then, Gwen?" Anger was bubbling up inside of him. Anger at his father. Anger at Gwen for making him face his ghosts.

"I suggest you put your rules aside, at least for tonight, and allow me to help you heal." She wiped the residual tears from his cheeks.

He was ashamed of his emotional outburst. "I'm sorry, Gwen. I've never cried like that before. I don't know what came over me."

"Well then, I'm so glad your first time was with me." She pressed a tender kiss to his forehead. "What came over you was a lifetime of being strong in the face of tragedy, pain, and abuse. Those scars that I felt on your back, were those put there by your father?"

He nodded. Benson had left a few, but he wasn't to blame. It was all his father's doing. Ash sucked in a shuddering breath as he suddenly understood, that's what Gwen had been saying about him and his actions.

"Those injuries on your back have healed, but the damage he did to your soul, that has been hidden away, still raw and bleeding. Perhaps tonight can be the first step in allowing those wounds to heal, as well."

"Why do you show me so much kindness, Gwen?"

"I learned that from you."

He jerked back.

"Is that really so hard to believe, Ash? You've only ever shown me kindness, even in my darkest hours. Even when I've poked, prodded, and teased you. Even this very night, you sacrificed your own wants and needs to ensure my greedy desires."

"If you're talking about what happened on the piano, that was certainly not a hardship."

"Wasn't it?" She reached between them, her hand gently settling against his trousers. His arousal immediately stirred at her soft caress. He grabbed her wrist and shook his head.

"Do you trust me, Ash?"

For a moment, he didn't answer. "Yes, but I don't trust me."

"Well, I do trust you, and I want to feel this inside me." She rubbed her hand against his growing erection. "I want to feel that connection. I want you to vanquish my dark memories of that act, and I want you to allow me to vanquish yours."

His breathing accelerated as a combination of panic and excitement warred within him. Could he really make love to her? Could he allow himself to forget about his past transgressions, just for a night? He'd certainly like to make her forget about her past.

"Are you really certain, Gwen?"

Joy radiated, like rays of sunshine, from the smile that grew on her face. "I've never been more certain of anything in my life."

"I don't know, Gwen."

"Well, why don't we try? And if you want to stop at any time, you can just say the word hairpin."

Laughter bubbled up from somewhere deep inside him.

She climbed off of his lap and held out her hand. They were really going to do this. He was really going to do this.

CHAPTER
TWELVE

After so many years, the prospect was daunting. It was somehow both terrifying and exhilarating. Gwen trusted him, and although he wasn't sure he was deserving of that trust, he had faith in her judgment.

He took the hand she offered and allowed her to lead him across the room to the bed.

"It's alright, Ash." She smiled up at him and squeezed his hand before turning to face the bed. She bent over and laid the top of her body across the bed. It took a moment for him to understand, but when he did, it was like a knife being plunged into his gut. She'd never known any other way. His eyes slid shut as he breathed in deeply through his nose. His heart broke, seeing her bent over the bed, expecting he was just going to take her.

He rubbed a gentle caress over her back. "Stand up, Gwen," he said, softly. "That's not how we're going to do this." She straightened and turned to face him, her cheeks stained with pink.

"Do you want me somewhere else?" Her eyes darted around the room.

He hooked a finger under her chin to get her eyes on him. "I want you right here, Angel." He lowered his lips to hers, kissing her tenderly. She responded with quick passion, taking the lead and plunging her tongue into his mouth. Dear God. He'd once again intended to take it slowly, but that seemed to be impossible with her. Her eagerness sparked his own passion. Soon, their tongues were dueling, a seductive dance of give and take.

"I need to feel your skin against mine," he said breathlessly, slipping the buttons open on his shirt.

She nodded fervently and untied her sash, shrugging out of her robe allowing it to pool on the floor. She stood gloriously naked before him, and his damn buttons weren't cooperating. He ripped the shirt the rest of the way and flung the garment onto the floor. He wrapped his arms around her, crushing her against him. A groan issued from his lips. The softness of her breasts pressed against his chest sent desire coursing through his veins. As his lips trailed along her neck, his hands explored every inch of her he could reach. Her skin was delectable, and the round globes of her backside, both firm and soft as he squeezed them. How could he instantly be so needy? His loins throbbed with desire.

Her small hands slid between them, fiddling with the fastening of his trousers. He stepped away from her. "We have to do the shoes first." He sat on the side of the bed and quickly untied his boots and kicked them off.

He placed his hands on his trousers. "Are you still sure you want this, Gwen?"

She tilted her head exasperatedly. "Yes."

A moment later, he was completely naked, and feeling surprisingly vulnerable as her eyes swept over his body. Tentatively, she placed her fingertips to his chest, her lips following shortly behind.

"I've never really... May I?" She didn't seem to be able to complete her question, but he understood. Somehow, she'd never seen a man fully naked and wanted to explore.

"You may do whatever your heart desires."

With an appreciative smile, she stepped back, just far enough to see properly, but still close enough to touch. Her fingertips brushed over his ribs, stopping at a scar that snaked around from the back. She leaned down and pressed a kiss to it. His stomach did a strange sort of flutter. The gesture shook loose a haze of confusing emotions.

Slowly, she made her way around his body, her fingers never leaving his skin. She didn't gasp or step away in horror at the sight of his gruesome back. Nearly every inch was covered with ugly, raised scars, from his shoulders to his knees. Instead, she wrapped her arms around his waist and pressed herself against the length of his back, the side of her face resting between his shoulder blades. She didn't move, or speak. Her breath fanned over his skin as she tried to take away the pain of his past.

Slowly, she pressed gentle kisses across his back, starting at his shoulder and zigzagging her way down. She didn't stop when she reached his bottom and he sucked in a breath as her lips pressed against the exposed skin. He closed his eyes, his heart stuttering at the intimacy of what she was doing. Somehow, it wasn't purely sexual, or even primarily so. Not that he wasn't still desperately hard with wanting. But what she was doing was so much more. Incredibly, she really was taking away his pain and his shame. His angel. She kissed all the way down to the few scars that striped across his calves before she eventually stood, once more.

She kissed her way around his shoulder to finally gaze up at him. "You're beautiful, Ash."

His instinct was to think she was teasing, but it was obvious she wasn't. How was that even possible? He'd seen the scars countless times in the mirror, and even he didn't like looking at them. "You don't think the scars are ugly?"

She shook her head. "I'm sorry for the pain you had to endure, but they are part of you. A reflection of your strength, a testament to all you've overcome. It's incredible that you've become such a kind, caring person, in spite of the horrible things that have been inflicted upon you."

He encircled her with his arms, drawing her against him again. Why did her closeness bring him so much comfort? He could happily hold her like this forever. But they didn't have forever. They only had tonight.

He claimed her lips, pouring his soul into her and taking whatever she would give in return. It really did feel as if their essences were connecting just as their mouths were. Overwhelmed, his heart galloped inside his chest as he gasped for breath. She whimpered as his fingers encased her breast. He flicked over the velvety tip with his thumb, and her body arched against him in response. He dipped his head, suckling briefly on the other nipple, and her fingers immediately gripped his hair. He smiled against her breast, flicking the nipple roughly with his tongue, and she squirmed, panting with need.

"Ash, I need more."

"You need me here?" He rested two fingers gently between her thighs.

"Yes!" Her voice was a harsh whisper. Wet heat surrounded his fingers as she rocked against him.

"Slow down, Angel."

She whined when he removed his fingers from between her legs. He pulled the blankets back and climbed underneath, patting the bed beside him. "Don't worry," he said as she slid in next to him. "I promise I'll take care of you."

He drew her nipple into his mouth. Never would he tire of the way she writhed with need from that simple act. He slipped his fingers between her legs, once more, and she groaned appreciatively. Slowly, he moved down to her entrance.

"May I?" He looked into her eyes and waited for her nod before he gently pressed a finger inside. She was so wet, so ready for him. He added a second finger and she groaned. An exquisite thrill filled his body, feeling her soft walls squeezing him.

Pushing himself up, he moved and settled himself between her legs, his tip nudging against her entrance. "Are you still sure?" he asked one last time.

"Ash! I'm desperate for it. Please."

"Thank God, because I am too." He was rewarded with a smile that conveyed so much happiness, but also something that looked like pride. It felt ridiculous that she would be proud of him for wanting this, and yet, he needed her to be.

Gently, he pressed himself into her body. My God, it was incredible. A look of shock came over her face. "Are you alright?" he asked.

"I didn't know it could feel like this, that it could be pleasurable."

"It only gets better from here," he said as he pulled out and plunged into her again. Jesus. How could anything feel so wondrous? After fourteen years of celibacy, this wasn't going to last long, but he was determined to hold out long enough to get her to the promised land, or die trying.

He crushed his lips to hers in a demanding kiss. Her moans filled his mouth as her pleasure grew. The amorous sounds made his own passions burn even hotter.

She was wonderfully expressive, panting needy groans with her burgeoning pleasure. Her fingers dug into his shoulders.

"Oh, God. Ash."

Her encouraging words and sounds made it nearly impossible for him to hold on. His own pleasure on a razor's edge.

"That's it, Angel. Come for me."

Her eyes grew wide and she nodded frenziedly, somehow understanding words that must be foreign to her. Her voice escalated and then she shouted to the heavens. She writhed beneath him, her body contracting around him. He carried her through her pleasure as long as he could manage before he had to wrench himself out of her. A feral roar ripped from deep inside him as his own climax claimed him. Violent spasms tore through him, his seed spilling over her thigh. His arms shook, barely able to hold his weight. When the spasms finally eased, he collapsed beside her.

He allowed himself a moment to recover, but he needed to get her cleaned up. With a herculean effort, he threw the blankets back and climbed off the bed.

"Wait," she called after him. "Don't leave me."

"I'm not leaving, Angel." He bent down and kissed her softly. "I'll be right back."

He walked to his dressing room and quickly wet a cloth. "I'm sorry it's cold."

She gasped quietly as he placed the damp cloth on her thigh. He gently cleaned the mess from her skin, and then wiped the cloth lightly between her legs, for good measure. "There. All clean."

He deposited it in his dressing room before climbing back into the warm bed. He pulled her tightly against him, her bottom nestled against his groin. He draped one arm over her, settling his palm over her breast. Her soft giggle warmed his heart.

"That was the most amazing thing I've ever experienced." Her voice was hoarse, and the knowledge that he'd brought her the pleasure that caused it to be that way, stroked his ridiculous ego.

"And me." He was still out of breath.

"You don't have to lie to make me feel better, you know." He could practically hear her eyes roll.

He bit her shoulder playfully. "Oh, I'm not lying,

Gwen. I've never experienced anything so powerful in all my life." He kissed the spot he'd bitten. "You, my angel, are incredible."

How in God's name was he going to give this up?

A long silence fell before she spoke again. "You know, you never did tell me about Trent."

Ash chuckled. "I'm afraid I'm not capable of that many words just now. Why don't we save that conversation for tomorrow's train ride?"

"Fair enough." She snuggled herself more tightly against him, placing her own hand over the one that covered her breast.

"Mmmmm. Sleep tight, Angel."

———

The next morning, Ash woke before dawn. He felt guilty slipping out of bed and leaving Gwen to wake up alone, but he had countless things to take care of before they could leave. Not to mention, if he stayed in bed, he'd want to make love to her again, and that couldn't happen. As incredible as the night had been, it was over. It was time for them to return to Raven House, and to their lives as employer and employee, once more. Somehow.

He wrote a quick note and left it on the pillow beside her. Hopefully that would help some. "Goodbye, my angel," he whispered as he looked down at her in the darkness. Next, it was time to dress and face his first task. He let out a sigh as he rang for Benson.

"Good morning, my lord. You're looking well."

"This scruffy face would suggest otherwise." He rubbed his hand over his bristly chin.

"Well then, let's get you shaved, shall we?"

Ash sat down and Benson draped a towel under his chin and around his neck. "I want to thank you, Benson. It has been a pleasure having you take care of me these few days."

"I assure you, my lord, it has been my honor." Ash would miss Benson. Fogg was a fine valet and served him well, but Benson looked at Ash as a loving father might.

"It's time for me to head back to London today, but I'm hoping you might consider staying on here in my absence. I don't know whether Trent would allow you to act as valet for him. He's certainly never had a manservant, and I believe his independence and stubbornness will make him refuse. But I'd like it if you could try to keep an eye on him and report to me."

His brow furrowed. "Like a spy, my lord?"

"No. I just want to know that he's taken care of mostly. He's never had a father, and I think he could use someone around who can impart gentle wisdom."

"I'm not sure it's my place, my lord, and I doubt I'm the best source for wisdom."

"All I know is that these past few days have made me wish I'd had a man like you as my father."

"I'd be proud if you were my son, Master Adrian." Tears glistened in the man's eyes.

Benson removed the towel and Ash stood. He placed a firm hand on the older man's shoulder. "You're a good man, Benson. Will you take me up on my offer?"

"I'd be honored to, my lord."

When Ash was dressed, Benson handed him his cane, with not so much as a raised eyebrow. Apparently, someone had found it on the piano where he'd left it.

"Thank you. You've saved me a trip down the stairs without it."

Who would ever have thought that coming back to this awful place would give Ash the opportunity to begin to heal his crippled soul? As he made his way across the house to find Trent, he could almost feel that the shattered pieces of his heart had begun to put themselves back together again.

He eventually found Trent in the nursery with Maggie. The pair of them were sitting in a circle with a couple of dolls, apparently enjoying a lovely tea. It was about time there was some life in this old house. Perhaps a bit of laughter and joy would help to chase away some of the shadows.

Maggie's eyes lit when she spotted him in the doorway. "Uncle Ash! Come and join us for tea!"

He chuckled. "I'd be honored to."

"Good morning," Trent said, as Ash lowered himself

to the floor. There was something off, a coldness that hadn't been there the last time they'd spoken.

"Good morning, Trent. I trust you slept well."

"You have to hold it like this," Maggie interrupted before Trent could answer. She modeled how to properly hold the teacup, her little pinky sticking up.

Ash laughed. "Like this?"

She nodded approvingly at his attempt, followed by a round of giggles. He'd miss her. It seemed strange that such a thing could be possible, considering he hadn't even known she existed a few days ago.

After a short time, Ash got to his feet and rang for a servant to watch over Maggie.

By the time he and Trent were settled into Ash's study, his concern had grown immensely. Trent hadn't spoken a single word to him other than his initial greeting.

"What's bothering you, Trent? Are you having some reservations?"

He shrugged. "Perhaps I am."

"If this is going to work,"—Ash gestured between the two of them—"we're going to have to be up front and honest with each other. If you need something, or if you have concerns, you're just going to have to tell me."

"Very well." His mouth was set in a grim line. "I believe you have misrepresented yourself."

The accusation made Ash a bit irritable. "I'm going to need more than that, Trent."

"Well, last night, I couldn't sleep, so I decided to do a bit of wandering." His eyes met Ash's, and there was loathing within them. "I saw you with Gwen."

Ash nodded and let out a long sigh. "Whatever you think that was, I can promise you it wasn't."

Trent huffed a cynical laugh. "I'm not a complete fool, Ash. After all your talk of no one touching the women who work for you. Especially you." He rolled his eyes. "I heard the pair of you in the ballroom and then I watched you carry her up the stairs. I think we can both agree that you weren't giving her piano lessons in there."

Ash sat back in his chair and folded his arms across his chest. If this were anyone else, he'd just punch them in their impertinent face and be done with it, but Trent needed to understand or he would never trust him.

"Well, up front and honest it is. When you are,"—Ash held out his hands, indicating his ownership of everything around them—"there is never a time when you are not in a position of power. If she's an employee, if she works in a brothel, even a mistress, they are all subordinate in some way. It took me a few years of being away from this place to really understand that. Once I did, I stopped allowing myself those types of interactions. I set strict rules for myself, sure that if I didn't have them, I'd inevitably become my father who took whatever he wanted, from whomever he wanted. Because of that, I've been celibate for fourteen years."

Trent's brow was furrowed, his eyes scouring Ash's face, but he didn't ask any questions, so Ash continued.

"As for Gwen, she has spent the past year believing herself to be married to someone who was, well, probably a lot like my father, actually. She has since discovered that was all a lie, after enduring a year of unspeakable abuse." Ash looked into Trent's eyes. "So what you witnessed last night was not me taking advantage of a subordinate. It was two very damaged people, trying to help one another to heal. Today, we are returning to Raven House where she will once again be my employee and my rules will be firmly back in place."

Trent nodded, his eyes glazing over a bit as his thoughts turned inward. After a moment, he met Ash's gaze. "I'm sorry, Ash. I shouldn't have made assumptions. But since we're being upfront and honest, perhaps you'll allow me to share some of my own story as an explanation."

"By all means. I'd love to know anything about your life that you're willing to share."

"The truth is, I feel as if we may be kindred spirits in some ways. You see, I am also celibate for the same kinds of reasons. Although, I've never actually... well..." His eyes flicked up to Ash's probably expecting some kind of ridicule, but when there was none, he continued. "My mother sometimes had to give favors to men in order to keep a roof over our heads. That's how Maggie came to be." He shrugged. "I've just never wanted to be one of those men, the predators who took advantage of my mother." He let out a long sigh.

"I'm sorry I wasn't able to help your mother, Trent."

He nodded, sadness settling on his face. "Anyway, I suppose that's why I immediately thought the worst when I saw you with Gwen, and I'm sorry."

"No need to apologize. There was no reason you should have thought any differently." Ash gave him a sad smile. "We're quite the pair, you and I. I guess we truly are brothers."

They shared a laugh. Trent was a good man, and Ash was grateful to suddenly have him in his life.

"You're young, though. There's hope for you yet. Perhaps once you settle into your role here, you can find yourself a lovely wife."

"One can only hope, I suppose. And what of you?"

Ash flicked his hand through the air waving the idea aside. "I'm going back to my life as a perpetual bachelor, running my club, making money, growing my little empire. It's enough to keep me busy."

"Somehow I have my doubts it will go that way." There was a bit of teasing in Trent's raised brow.

"What does that mean?"

"Well, all due respect, but I think you're being naive to believe everything is just going to go back to the way it was. I'm no expert on the subject, but I saw the way you looked at Gwen as you carried her up the stairs. Even in the dark it was obvious you are completely besotted."

Ash shook his head. Trent wasn't wrong. Of course he was besotted, but that didn't matter. "I don't have that luxury."

"Well, good luck, then."

Ash barked a laugh. He was going to need all the luck he could get.

"On to other business. I wanted to talk to you about Benson, the man who's been acting as my valet while I've been here. I've asked him to stay on here and keep an eye on things. He will be at your disposal if you need anything."

"One of your spies?"

"It's funny you should say that, because that's exactly what he said when I asked him to keep an eye on you. These past few days, Benson has been a caring, fatherly kind of figure to me, and I have truly appreciated it. I think you could probably use that, as well. He has a lot of wisdom to impart and warmth to share." Ash shrugged. "I hope one day you'll even allow him to act as a valet for you." He could see Trent gearing up to argue, so he held up a hand to stop him.

"I know you're not ready for that, and maybe you never will be, but when you have a good valet, they can become a bit of a confidante. A friendly face at the end of a rotten day. Benson is a good man, and you can trust him."

Trent pondered quietly for a moment. "Thank you. I

suppose I hadn't ever really thought of any of that. I'll be sure to talk to him."

"Good. Now, I have one other thing to take care of before I go. I need to address the staff, and I'd like it if you were there, as well, so that I can introduce you formally."

Trent blew out a long breath.

"Don't worry," Ash assured him. "They don't bite."

THIRTEEN

When Gwen woke, she knew before she even opened her eyes that she was alone in the bed. Ash's warmth wasn't there, and she already missed it. There was a piece of paper on the pillow beside hers.

Gwen,

I'm sorry I left you, but I have a lot to take care of before our departure. You needn't worry about anything, so enjoy a warm bath and take your time getting ready.

Ash

No 'Angel'. He wasn't only gone from the bed, he was gone from her. Even though she'd known it was coming, her heart still broke. She wouldn't cry, or fall to pieces. If he knew she was hurting, he'd blame himself, so she steeled herself, threw back the blanket, and climbed out of his bed for the last time.

She did order herself a hot bath. She wasn't about to pass up the opportunity for one more soak in that luxurious tub. Her inner thigh muscles ached slightly as she lowered herself into the steamy, fragrant water, likely from all the shaking they'd done the night before. As she washed between her legs, she could still feel him there, and remembered what it was like having him buried deep inside her. She would cherish every memory she had of their time together here.

When she eventually made her way down the main staircase, there was a line of servants filing into the ballroom. *The* ballroom. She stood, frozen in place on the stairs until long after the last person disappeared into the room. After a few minutes, determined to not allow her pain to show, she straightened her spine and quietly slipped through the door.

Ash stood before the entire group, a commanding presence as his deep voice filled the room.

"I'd like to introduce you all to Mr. Gibson. He is—" His head whipped to the side, his gaze immediately locking on her. The slightest hint of a smile graced his lips. He had smelled her. She blushed with the realization and the memory of exactly what had occurred on that piano he now stood in front of.

He shook his head as if to clear it. "Mr. Gibson will be overseeing the estate in my absence and he will be in residence. If you need anything, or have anything to report, he will be available to you. One thing I'd like to make clear is that things are going to be very different around here moving forward. I want every person here to feel safe in this house. If any of you ever feel unsafe, from anyone, that includes Mr. Gibson, any other staff or visitors, anyone, I want you to report it immediately. You may bring it to the attention of Mrs. Archer, Mr. Moulton, Mr. Gibson, or directly to me. I will ensure that each and every one of you has my direction so that you may reach out to me via post or telegram. Your safety and happiness are of the utmost importance to me. Is that clear?"

There was a chorus of "Yes, my lord," from the servants. A few of the women breathed a sigh of relief, but most of them seemed unsure of what to think about the pronouncement.

"As a thank you for your loyalty even in my absence, you will all be receiving bonuses." Gwen watched all of their faces brighten. Pride blossomed inside her chest. In order to improve the lives of the people who worked for him, he was making a permanent connection with this place, even though it was the source of so many nightmares. Of course, none of them would ever know that. Benson was probably the only other person here to ever see his scars, and she was the only one to hold his shaking body when he awoke from a night terror. She didn't blame him for leaving this place as quickly as possible, even if she wished they could stay forever.

The long train ride was pleasant, if a little awkward. At first, it was obvious they both had pasted on smiles, but eventually, they settled into comfortable conversation. He told her all about Trent and his vision for the estate moving forward. They talked of the weather. They talked of the changes that had taken place at Raven House since last she was there. Apparently, both Patrick and Michael had married, and Patrick's mother-in-law now acted as surrogate mother and manager to all of the ladies. It was hard to believe those two men had married. All three of them had been decided bachelors, as far as Gwen had always known. Although, according to Ash, Michael had actually been betrothed the whole time. There was also a new addition to the group of partners, named Giles. Perhaps all the changes would make it easier to return.

What they didn't discuss were all of the wonderful things that had happened between them over the last few days. It couldn't continue, no matter how much she wished it could, so there was no point in dwelling or reminiscing. Although, she did wonder if he, too, was sad to see it end.

When the hired hack pulled up to the backdoor of Raven House, Ash helped her to step down. It was one of the few times they'd made physical contact during the journey, and even with gloves on, it sent a thrill through her. Their eyes met briefly before he quickly looked away.

It was dark, but the porte cochere was lit by two lamps. Her breath created clouds as it left her lips, which was strangely comforting. It was as if the cold outside somehow offset the cold that had settled around her heart.

As she looked up at the entrance to Raven House a mass of emotions fought for her attention. She was frightened, of course. Not because this was new. She'd obviously been here before. But the last time, it had been a refuge, a stepping stone to help her to a better life. She'd certainly managed to muck that up. She felt like a naughty child being sent back to school.

A large man Gwen didn't recognize held the door for them. Probably someone who had been hired since last she was here.

"Welcome home, boss. We didn't expect you back so quickly."

"Neither did I, but everything went smoothly."

It was a change to have him back to boss instead of my lord. Another reminder that things were back to the way they had been once before.

The moment they walked through the door, someone shouted. "Gwen? Is it really you?"

Gwen couldn't help but return Daisy's excited smile. "I'm like a bad penny," she said with a shrug. Daisy squealed and threw her arms around her.

"I can't believe it! Are you staying?" She didn't wait for an answer before turning her sights on Ash.

"If she's staying, she's in my room." She pointed a demanding finger at him.

Ash held up his hands. "Whatever you say, Daisy."

He had such an easy way with all of the ladies here. Was it possible they could fall back into that again?

"I'm running late, so I have to dash, but it's the last door on the left. Make yourself at home." She gave Gwen another quick hug and bussed her cheek before disappearing up the stairs.

At least she had been greeted by a friendly face. Daisy was such a lovely person. It was a surprise to see her still here, but a welcome one. Gwen would be happy to share a room with her.

"I thought I heard a commotion out here." A woman entered the main area from the hall that housed all of the ladies' chambers.

"Ah, Sarah. Gwen, this is Sarah. I told you about her on the train. Sarah, this is Gwen. She's not new here, but she has been away for about eighteen months or so. Will you please help her to settle in? Daisy has demanded that she stay with her."

Sarah's smile was warm and welcoming. "Of course I will, Ash. Don't you worry about a thing."

Sarah escorted her to Daisy's room and fretted over her for at least a quarter hour before Gwen finally managed to convince her that she was fine and not in need of anything. The moment the door closed behind Sarah and Gwen was finally alone, her smile fell. The dam that had been holding back her burgeoning emotions all day, suddenly gave way. And as if it had been the only thing keeping her upright, her legs crumpled with it and she collapsed to the floor as sobs broke from her. A tidal wave of grief washed over her.

Her heart ached with a kind of pain she didn't even know existed. How was she possibly going to survive this?

———

Ash breathed in deeply as the smells and sounds of the Raven's Den welcomed him home. A cacophony of noise and the aroma of all that accompanied it. Booze, cards, tobacco smoke, clay chips, he could smell them all. For most people, it would be an assault to the senses, but for Ash, it was home.

Michael stood on the balcony watching over the gaming floor below. "I'm gone less than a week and already you have ladies running late for their shifts?"

Michael swung around, his face bright with surprise and delight. "Ash! We didn't expect you back so soon."

As he moved closer, Michael's delight faltered. "Jesus, man. Is everything alright?"

Ash nodded. "Everything is taken care of. I'm glad to be home."

Michael's eyebrows rose inquiringly. "That's it?"

Ash chuckled. "I'm tired and there's a lot to tell. I'd rather only do it once, at tomorrow's meeting. I just came over to make sure the club was still standing. It looks like you have it well in hand."

"Of course we do. Now go get some sleep. You look like you've just risen from the dead."

Ash could barely even laugh at the remark. "I imagine I do."

"Get some rest, Ash. I want you well enough to give a full account tomorrow."

"You might be sorry you asked for it." He gave Michael a half-hearted salute with his cane and headed back the way he'd come in.

Fogg was standing in his bedroom when he entered a few minutes later. "You're a welcome sight. I wasn't sure if you'd be here tonight, but thank God you are. I'm not sure I have the energy to even undress myself."

"Of course I'm here."

"I didn't think you'd know I was coming home tonight."

"Knowing where you are is the most important part of my job, Ash."

"I'm not sure what I've done to deserve the amazing people I have around me, but I am grateful to all of you."

"Well, to the rest of us, it's obvious you're deserving. Now, let's get you ready for bed. You look like you're ready to drop where you stand."

"Any news?" Ash asked, as Fogg helped him to undress.

"Not yet, but we'll find him, Ash."

He was growing impatient. He wanted to make the man suffer for hurting Gwen. His angel. He couldn't seem to stop thinking of her that way. But she wasn't his, in any way, anymore.

His bed was cold without her in his arms and he was agitated. He'd seen her sadness. Oh, she'd tried her best to hide it from him, to spare him from the guilt she'd known he would feel. But he could see it, a shadow deep in her eyes, the sparkle growing less bright as the day went on and they traveled farther away from Woodburn Hall. He'd wanted to hold her and tell her everything was going to be alright. But that was one of the few things he simply couldn't do, and it killed him inside. He had so much power and so many connections. He could move mountains when he brought all of his resources to bear, but he couldn't give her what she needed.

She needed someone who was whole. Someone who wasn't scarred inside and out. Someone who was respectable and didn't own a gaming hell. Someone who wasn't him. And yet, the thought of her with someone else, grated at his heart and turned his stomach. He rolled over and pounded a fist into his pillow. Maybe it didn't matter. She'd said she didn't want to marry again, and perhaps she wouldn't.

He sat up in bed, his elbows on his knees, fingers

gripped into his hair. Sleep was not going to happen, regardless of how tired he was. As he felt the scars stretch tight across his back, his mind replayed the events of last night. Was it really just last night? He could still feel her soft lips against his skin. Her tender affection helping his heart to begin to heal. But now it was breaking all over again. He sighed.

Something had to break, so it might as well be his heart. It could not be his will.

FOURTEEN

Somehow, Gwen had slept right through Daisy's return in the early hours of the morning. The sun was shining brightly around the edges of the curtains. The blanket covered every inch of Daisy except for her nose. Even her eyes were covered. They'd all gotten good at blocking out the light for their strange sleeping hours. She'd have to readjust to that now that she'd be working nights again.

It was hard to believe she was here again. She was trying her best to reconcile everything that had happened. Until just a few days ago, she had thought herself married. Miserable, but married. She'd thought herself in love with Greg before they'd wed, but the feelings she'd had for him, even then, were nothing compared to what had blossomed with Ash. If she was honest with herself, she'd always wanted Ash, from the day he'd rescued her from the streets. He'd never allowed anything to happen between them and had treated her just like all of the other ladies here. That hadn't stopped her from trying, though. She'd always been a bit of a flirt with him. She wouldn't be able to do that anymore. For both of their sakes, she would have to be on her best behavior.

Quietly, she changed into clean clothes, careful to not wake Daisy. Closing the door softly behind her, she went in search of food and tea. Her stomach rumbled loudly in protest at being empty too long.

When Gwen entered the main hall, she was surprised to see Patrick, and even more surprised to see his arms wrapped around a woman, his hands clasping her bottom while he kissed her passionately. Patrick also treated all the ladies respectfully and never crossed any boundaries, so it was strange to see him that way. She wasn't sure what to do. Part of her brain said to turn back and not interrupt, but the drawing room with the food was on the other side of them. In the end, she just stood there, her eyes darting around awkwardly, trying not to stare at the pair of them.

"Oh!" Patrick said suddenly. "Apologies, I didn't realize anyone was around." He stopped then, and really looked at her. "Gwen? What are you doing here?" His brow was furrowed with concern.

Gwen shrugged. "I'm back," she said quietly.

He walked away from the woman he'd been kissing,

hopefully his wife, and approached Gwen. "Are you alright?"

She nodded. "I'm just headed to the drawing room in search of some tea and something to put in my stomach." She turned her lips up in a smile that she hoped was reassuring.

"Oh, of course. I'm sorry to be in the way." Then, as an afterthought he continued, "Gwen, this is my wife, Rosie."

"It's nice to meet you, Rosie." She didn't seem to be able to muster the strength for another smile, so she simply nodded.

Rosie, on the other hand, beamed at her. "Do you mind if I join you? We've just arrived, and you know how train tea is." She shook her head, making a sarcastic face of disgust and sticking out her tongue. The joke brightened Gwen's outlook just a bit. Perhaps the company would do her good.

"That would be lovely, thank you."

Rosie touched her hand to the side of the teapot and her lips scrunched to one side in disapproval. "That won't do."

But just then, a housekeeper bustled in with a new pot. "Mrs. Corstairs, you are an angel."

Gwen's stomach clenched at the word and she closed her eyes, trying to center herself before she spiraled into uncontrollable grief, once more. She took a deep steadying breath.

"Do you take sugar?"

When she realized Rosie was talking to her, she wrenched her eyes open and tried to focus. "Pardon?"

Rosie smiled kindly. "Never mind. This is definitely a time for sweet tea."

Gwen tried to return the smile, but it just wouldn't come.

Rosie prepared their tea and handed one to Gwen. She placed her hand on Gwen's wrist and crouched in front of her. "I'm sorry for whatever you're going through." There was such understanding in her eyes. "If you want to talk about it, I'm happy to listen. Or if you want to pretend nothing is happening, I can do that too." She squeezed her arm lightly before settling into her own chair.

Tears burst from Gwen's eyes and she set the cup and saucer on the table with a clatter. Stupid tears. "I'm sorry," she said as she swept them away. "I didn't mean to start crying."

Rosie relocated to sit beside Gwen on the settee. She wrapped an arm around her and pulled her head against her shoulder. "No need to apologize, dear. You cry out all your grief." She rocked her gently, but Gwen pulled herself together. What if Ash came down and saw her this way? Or what if Patrick saw her and told Ash?

She sniffled and sat back, wiping the remainder of her tears away. "Please don't tell Ash I was crying."

Rosie looked taken aback. "Is Ash back?"

Gwen nodded. "We got here last night."

"And why do you not want him to know you've been crying? You realize he's seen all of us crying, don't you?"

"Us? Were you a Lady Raven?"

Rosie's smile returned. "Not exactly, but I did live here for a short time. Why don't I tell you my story while you drink this." She handed the tea back to Gwen. "And then, you can share yours."

Gwen closed her eyes at the overwhelming sweetness of the tea.

Rosie smiled. "I know, but Ella swears it's good for soothing a troubled soul, so drink up."

Rosie went on to tell an incredible story about Patrick saving her from a brothel, and then a whole topsy-turvy journey that followed, that included her being rescued by Ash. "So as you can imagine, Ash has seen me at my worst. He's never judged me for a moment, and he wouldn't judge you either."

Gwen let out a long sigh that sounded tortured, even to her own ears. After Rosie had been so candid with everything she'd been through, it felt churlish for Gwen to refuse to share her own story. She decided to tell parts of it, but she would never reveal Ash's secrets. They were not hers to share. She explained how Ash had found her and the fake marriage she'd been foolish enough to fall for. "Without getting into any of Ash's personal details, I'll just say that, even knowing I shouldn't, I fell in love with him. If he knows that I'm hurting, he'll blame himself, and I don't want him to feel guilty." Gwen ended with a slightly pathetic shrug.

Although Rosie's eyes held obvious sympathy, there was a hint of mischief there too. "Well, you must be something special. I never thought I'd see the day that someone would break through Ash's unyielding rules."

"I didn't say anything about his rules." Had she betrayed him even though she'd tried not to?

Rosie smiled reassuringly. "You didn't have to, dear. But don't worry, I won't say anything to him."

"As you can imagine, I just don't know quite what to do."

"Well, for now, you just have to keep putting one foot in front of the other. If there's one thing I know about these stubborn men it's that you can't convince them to do anything. They just have to figure it out on their own. Until then, anytime you need to get away from this place for a little while, you're more than welcome to visit me. I'm sure Belle, Michael's wife, would love to have you, as well."

"That's so kind of you."

By the time Patrick returned to collect Rosie, the evidence of Gwen's crying had hopefully disappeared. Rosie gave her a hug. "I'll send Belle to introduce herself. We're not often both in town at the same time, but one of us is usually around. When you need something, just have the doorman send a note to one of us and we'll appear."

"You're too kind, Rosie."

"Don't be silly." She waved away the sentiment. She squeezed her hands one last time. "Take care of yourself."

What had she meant when she'd said 'they just have to figure it out on their own'? Figure what out? Gwen didn't understand, but she was grateful for the conversation and for Rosie's kindness. She had assured her multiple times that everything would be alright and things would work themselves out somehow in the end.

Now, if only Gwen could make herself believe that were true.

———

Ash was jarred awake by a sudden onslaught of blinding light.

"I had to come check you're alive," Fogg said as he threw back the other set of curtains.

Ash groaned. His head throbbed painfully. He seemed to be on his stomach, spread like a starfish across his entire bed, and he didn't feel a stitch of clothing on his skin. He must have presented quite a sight. "Can you be a little more quiet please?" he whispered.

He heard Fogg's intake of breath and braced for the loud noises, but none came. Ash flopped his head over on the bed and squinted up at his valet. "What did I say about walking on eggshells?"

"Rough night?" Fogg raised a brow as he appraised

the scene Ash presented. Ash huffed a laugh and quickly groaned again as his head protested.

"You might say that." He'd eventually drunk himself to sleep.

"Well, since I'm not walking on eggshells, might it be because you didn't have a certain lady warming your bed last night?"

"That wasn't permission for you to be impertinent." Ash glared at the man. "I'd ask how you even know about that since you weren't there, but somehow you always know every bloody thing."

"It's not exactly a secret, Ash. Your entire household at Woodburn is aware that she was in your bed every night you stayed there. The difference is, they don't know how unusual that is for you. As far as they were concerned, she was your mistress. It would have been strange if she hadn't been in your bed."

Ash slowly pushed himself upright. He sat on the edge of the bed and scrubbed his hands over his face.

"I'm concerned about you, Ash. You've never once had a woman in your bed, the entire time I've been in your employ. You go to Woodburn Hall, and you have Gwen in your bed from the first night you arrive?"

"Yes, well, I'm back here now so that's obviously not going to happen again. Now please tell me you brought coffee."

"Of course I did," he said, pouring a cup and handing it to him.

Ash took the cup and breathed in the wonderful aroma. "I could kiss you."

Fogg grimaced. "I'd rather you didn't, if it's all the same."

Ash glared at him, but he simply shrugged. "Well how am I supposed to be sure you won't? Everything seems to be changing with you all of a sudden."

Ash chuckled and shook his head. "You are an impudent arse, Fogg."

"Would his lordship like to dress at some point today? It is past one, after all."

"Christ." He let out an aggravated sigh and took a large gulp of the hot coffee. "I need you to work your magic, Fogg. If Michael, Patrick, and Giles see me looking like this, they'll be worse than you with their fretting."

"I'll certainly do my best, but I've never seen you look quite so..." His words trailed off and he simply tilted his head to the side.

Laughter surprised him. "Thanks, Fogg." Ash was glad Fogg was back to his usual bantering. He'd feared their relationship might have changed at Woodburn as well.

A short while later, as Fogg was fastening the buttons on his waistcoat, Ash was feeling, and looking, much more himself. "I'm sure this goes without saying, Fogg, but what happened between Gwen and me at Woodburn, stays there. I don't need that kind of gossip spreading around here."

Fogg nodded. "It won't come from me, but I'm afraid those kinds of things have a habit of finding their way about anyway."

The familiar sensation of self-loathing burned in Ash's belly. "I'm a bloody fool," he muttered. He'd been naive believing they could come back to Raven House and everything would be just as it had been before. He'd likely damned Gwen to relentless speculation and gossip. All the ladies knew that he did not interact with them in a manner anything more than friendly and professional. If they learned that Gwen had been intimate with him, it would create all kinds of problems. "Christ." He plunged a hand into his hair.

"I just straightened that," Fogg admonished, but then he placed a gentle hand on Ash's shoulder. "I won't pretend to know what happened at Woodburn, but I know you, Ash. Whatever occurred, it came from a place of caring and compassion, not from malice."

"My good intentions will not spare her from the consequences of my actions."

"There is a way you could put it all to rest, you know."

Ash dreaded the answer, but asked the question anyway. "How?"

"Marry her."

Ash scoffed. "And damn her to a lifetime shackled to me? Not a chance. You just focus on finding the bastard who sent her back to me in the first place, so I can send him to hell where he belongs."

"You know we will."

An hour later, as Ash stood overlooking his club, his gaze was unfocused. Instead, words continued to play though his head. "Marry her." And then it would be followed immediately by Gwen's voice saying, "I don't think I ever want to marry again."

It didn't matter anyway. This is what he was, the owner of a gaming hell. He wasn't a husband. He wasn't someone a woman could settle down with and have a family. He didn't want that life. He didn't want to risk becoming his father. Although, as the thought settled in his mind, he knew it to be false. After spending only a short time with Maggie, he knew he could never harm any child. Perhaps the belief he'd held his entire life, the fear that he was his father's son and that the only thing keeping him from doing all the same, horrific things, was his strict set of rules. Perhaps that wasn't real. Perhaps there was no monster inside of him that he had to keep at bay.

His thoughts were interrupted by the sound of the backdoor closing. Patrick, Michael, and Giles all filed through the curtain onto the gaming floor. Michael looked up at him. "Are you going to join us?"

"Ash!" Giles said in surprise. "I didn't know you were back!"

Apparently Patrick did know, because he wasn't

surprised to see him. Ash made his way down the stairs. The pain in his leg was finally feeling a little better today, and he didn't have to rely on his cane as heavily. Michael and Giles brought all four of their drinks from the bar and set them around their usual table.

"Ash isn't the only one back," Patrick said as they settled into their seats. "Apparently Gwen arrived with him last night."

"How do you know that?" Ash asked, trying not to sound accusatory, but failing.

Patrick raised a questioning brow. "I saw her this morning when I came to check in and make sure all was well at Raven House. Was it supposed to be a secret?"

Ash's heart began to race. "What did she say?"

"Nothing. Not a single explanation." He looked at Ash. "I'm hoping you can provide that because she didn't look very happy, and they don't usually come back after that long away."

Ash breathed a sigh of relief and hated himself for it. "I think we're going to need to place her somewhere quickly. Somewhere I can trust she'll be safe. Do either of you have need of someone at an estate?" He looked at Patrick. "Or perhaps your brother?"

"I'm sure one of us could find room for her," Patrick replied. "But we're going to need more of an explanation than that, Ash."

Ash explained how he'd found her and told them

about the abusive fake marriage she'd been in for a year. All three of their faces grew horrified and then angry.

"Where is this piece of garbage?" Michael growled, his hands fisted on top of the table.

"I don't know yet, but I have good men working on that, and I will take care of him as soon as he's found."

"You mean *we* will take care of him," Michael said quietly. "These ladies are under all of our protection, Ash. Not just yours."

"Michael is right," Patrick added. "But there's still something you're not telling us. Why does she need to be placed somewhere? Why not keep her here, where we know she's safe, and looked after by all of the other ladies, and Sarah? Does she not want to be here?"

Ash closed his eyes, his stomach suddenly churning with nausea. "Because." He swallowed, steeling himself for what he needed to say. "While we were at Woodburn Hall, she shared my bed." Ash risked a glance up at his friends, expecting to see derision or anger. Instead, what he saw was shock. Except for Giles, who just looked confused. He hadn't been around long enough to fully understand the enormity of Ash's confession.

Patrick was the first one to finally speak. "You're serious?"

"It's not likely to be something I'd joke about. Is it?" Ash ripped out the words.

A group of sighs made their way around the table. Ash had a sudden need to justify, to explain his actions.

"Obviously I'm not going to go into any detail with the three of you, but believe me when I say this wasn't a case of me taking advantage of an employee. I swear nothing like that will ever happen with any of the other ladies. You can still trust me around them."

Michael threw back his head and laughed.

"I don't see what's so funny," Ash growled.

Michael shook his head. "Of course you don't. Ash, none of us thinks you've suddenly turned into a debaucher of young women. You've spent your entire adult life as sexually repressed as a monk."

"Michael isn't wrong, although perhaps a bit tactless in his description." Patrick threw a disappointed look toward Michael.

Michael held up his hands. "Fair enough. I'm sorry, Ash. I was only being sarcastic. But you must know that after all we've been through together, we trust you. Of all of us, you would be the last one to take advantage of any woman, let alone one under your protection."

Giles raised his hand a bit before speaking, as if he needed permission. "I know I'm the new guy here, and I don't know anything really, but is being placed quickly in a position somewhere what Gwen wants? I feel like that's the important question that no one seems to be asking."

Ash nodded grimly. "The truth is, I don't know. I don't see a good alternative, though. I think it would be naive to believe that gossip about what happened with

Gwen and me won't eventually make its way around Raven House. I hadn't really considered that until Fogg mentioned it this afternoon." How could he have been so stupid? "Christ!" He slammed his hands on the table, standing so forcefully that his chair tumbled over backwards. He picked up his mostly empty glass from the table and hurled it across the room, unleashing a string of curses.

"Hey," Patrick said sternly. "I know you're angry, but don't wreck the place. We have to open in just a couple of hours. Either pull yourself together or find somewhere else to have your temper tantrum."

Ash breathed in deeply. As much as he wanted to rage and destroy things, Patrick was right. It wasn't going to help.

He turned back to the table. "I'm sorry. It's been a trying few days, and somehow I've managed to create a right bloody mess for which Gwen will likely pay the consequences."

"Well, we are your friends and partners, so sit back down, and together, we'll figure out how best to move forward." It was almost amusing to have Patrick be the voice of reason, the one in charge. That was usually Ash, but he was grateful that the others were willing to step up and put him in his place when necessary.

As Ash righted his chair and sat back down, Michael spoke again. "I think Giles is right. You, or one of us, needs to have a conversation with Gwen to find out what it is she wants."

Ash nodded slowly. "It needs to be me."

FIFTEEN

When the other ladies got up for their shift, Gwen went back to her room to hide, grateful that she managed to miss Daisy. She just didn't have the strength to face them all yet. Most of them were probably new since she left all those months ago, but there would be a few that knew her. They'd wonder why she was back and what happened. She couldn't yet bring herself to tell the story of her marriage.

There was a light tap on the door and Sarah peeked her head in. "Good afternoon, Gwen." Her smile was kind and reassuring.

"Good afternoon, Sarah."

"Ash would like a word with you in his office."

Gwen's stomach clenched. It had been a long time since she was last summoned to the office. Usually, being summoned meant you were in for a lecture, but she hadn't even had a chance to earn one yet. Unless he somehow knew about her conversation with Rosie and was upset about it.

Gwen nodded and steeled herself before leaving the safety of her room and making her way to his office. He greeted her with the smile she remembered from her days as a Lady Raven. One that was kind and caring, but in no way hinted at any kind of attraction or desire.

"Come in, Gwen. Close the door and have a seat."

She did as she was told, the blessed numbness keeping her emotions steady as she looked at him across the desk.

"How are you faring?"

"Fine," she lied with a shrug. "It will be better once I'm working at night again. Less time to get bored."

He nodded, but he looked a bit distracted, as if he hadn't really listened to her answer because he was already thinking about what was coming next.

"What do you see your future looking like, Gwen?"

She felt a fracture form in the wall that was keeping her grief at bay, and anger seeped through. "I don't know, Ash. I just got back here last night, where I'm supposed to pretend like everything is perfectly normal after learning a mere few days ago that my one-year marriage was a sham, and the man I thought was my husband was only ever my abuser. That was followed by the most incredible few days I've ever experienced with a man who I can never actually have and who is now my boss once more. I don't think there's a guide for what comes next in this kind of scenario."

Ash looked as if he'd aged ten years in two days. His bloodshot eyes appeared slightly haunted with shadows lingering beneath and his brow furrowed as if he carried the weight of the world on his shoulders. He probably did, and rather than showing some kind of empathy, she'd snapped at him. None of this was his fault.

"I'm sorry, Ash. That wasn't fair of me."

"You've nothing to apologize for, Gwen. It was absolutely fair. I've been so selfishly wrapped up in what happened between us, sometimes I forget all you're dealing with on top of that. Perhaps I need to be completely upfront and stop being cryptic about what I'm really asking."

Suddenly, she understood. "Please don't send me away."

He closed his eyes, but she could still see the pain that settled on his face. When he opened them again, he gave a sad little laugh. "The words that got us into so much trouble."

She shook her head. "It wasn't trouble, Ash. Those nights were magical. A gift that I will never ever forget. I will treasure every second of the time I spent with you at Woodburn until I breathe my last breath. Please don't ever convince yourself that it was anything less."

His hands were gripped tightly together on top of his

desk and the muscles of his jaw were clenched. Eventually, he nodded.

"Do you not think it might be easier somewhere away from me? Perhaps you could even take a position at Woodburn Hall?"

She shot him a look of disbelief. "And relive our time together day after day?"

"No, of course, that was a stupid suggestion. But between Michael, Patrick, and Patrick's brother, one of them could certainly take you on. It would be a decent position where you'd be safe and looked after. They're all good men."

"I want to stay here, Ash."

"Before you make your decision, there is one other thing to consider. There is always the possibility that rumors of what happened between the two of us could eventually find their way here. That could change how you're treated by the others."

"I'm sure I can weather it. They're already going to know that I was bamboozled into a fake marriage. How much worse can it possibly be?"

"It could also cause problems for me. I'm afraid it would undermine my authority and my rules."

"Well, that may be true, but if the rumors are going to somehow appear here, that will happen whether I'm here or not."

"You're probably right." He looked so tired. Was he feeling heartbroken too?

"Is it hard for you to be around me, Ash? Is that why you want to send me away? Would it be easier for you if I go?"

"I don't know." His hand moved as if to reach across the desk, but he quickly pulled it back. "It's going to be an adjustment for us both. But if you wish to stay, I won't force you to leave. You'll always be welcome here, Gwen."

"Thank you. The truth is, I love it here. I love the life of the city. I love dancing in your club, surrounded by so much energy. I love being awake until the wee hours of the morning. The camaraderie of the women who live here. It feels more like home to me than anywhere else I've ever lived."

A genuine smile finally graced his lips. "I'm glad you love it here, Gwen."

"When can I start working?"

He shrugged. "I'll have a word with Sarah and Iris and let them know you're eager to get back to it."

———

Over the next couple of weeks, things did get a little easier. Dancing in the club gave her something to look forward to and a sense of accomplishment. All the ladies had been so welcoming. None of them had even asked her why she came back. Ash had probably asked them not to, which she was grateful for.

She'd also learned, if she returned to the stairwell after the club was closed and the other ladies had gone to bed, she could hear Ash playing his piano. That's where she was waiting tonight.

Just when she was about to give up and go to her room, notes began to float down to her. She climbed quietly up to the top step where she could be near the door that led to his private chambers. The music made her feel as if she had the tiniest connection to him that wasn't as his employee.

He didn't play for very long, and when the notes stopped and didn't start up again, she eventually returned to her room. The music played her to sleep inside her mind. She could almost convince herself that he was playing just for her.

She found herself looking forward to those moments more than anything else in her day. The few moments she could listen to him play. The next night was no different. She left the club with all the other ladies and changed out of her raven gown. When Daisy was asleep, she slipped back out to the staircase. She waited at the bottom of the steps until she heard him start to play. Once again, she crept up the stairs to the top.

The music always came straight from his soul. It told her how he was feeling, no walls or fake smiles, just truth. Tonight was mournful and his frustration came through when he struck the deep notes a little more forcefully. He was hurting. She needed to comfort him, and before she even thought, she was tapping softly on his door. The music stopped.

"Come." His voice was deep and laced with concern. No one ever bothered him in his private quarters, so he probably assumed there was a problem.

What was she doing? Her heart began to pound but she couldn't very well just run away now. She slowly opened the door and stepped through. His black hair was still damp from his bath, his robe open just enough to give her a glimpse of his bare chest as he sat before his piano.

"You can't be here, Gwen." He shook his head.

"I know," she said, butterflies taking flight inside her stomach. "I promise I won't do anything. I'll sit quietly. I won't say anything or come near you. I'll just listen."

"Gwen, we can't do this. It isn't right. You need to leave."

Her heart aching, she forced herself to accept his wishes and nodded her agreement. "I'll go, but please don't stop playing. I shouldn't have knocked. I'm sorry." Panic swept through her. She was going to lose this wonderful thing she had. Why did she have to knock on his door and ruin it? She was such a fool. "Please don't stop playing. Don't take this away from me. I promise I'll never knock again."

His chest was rising and falling as his breaths acceler-ated. "You've been listening to me out there?"

She didn't want to admit it, terrified that he'd stop

playing if he knew she was there, but she couldn't bring herself to lie to him. Slowly, she nodded. "It's my favorite part of the day. You play me to sleep every night." She met his gaze, her eyes pleading with him. "Please don't stop. I'll go."

She turned to leave, but in an instant, his fingers were wrapped around her upper arm. He pulled her against him and pushed the door closed as his lips slammed against hers. His tongue plunged roughly into her mouth as he backed her up and crushed her against the wall with his body.

"I don't know how to do this, Gwen. I've been desperate for you, and I don't know how to stop myself wanting you."

She nodded frenziedly. "Then take me. Please, Ash." She was panting in her need for him. "I want to feel you inside me again." He groaned and plundered her mouth, the evidence of his arousal pushing against her belly.

Frantic to have him, she began pulling up her nightgown. Without hesitation, he plunged his fingers between her legs, which she spread eagerly for him.

"My God, how can you already be so wet for me?" He slipped a finger inside her and she groaned her pleasure into his mouth.

She pulled open the sash of his black velvet robe and was delighted to see he wore nothing beneath. She wrapped her fingers around his swollen manhood and reveled in the feel of his hard length in her hand.

"I need this inside of me, Ash. Now."

"We shouldn't do this, Gwen."

"I don't care." She pumped her fist up and down and a groan caught in his throat. He grabbed her wrist and placed her hands on his shoulders. Lifting one of her legs to wrap around his waist, he settled his tip against her entrance.

"Are you sure you want this?"

"Yes." Her need was painful and she was desperate to have him fill her.

He grabbed her other leg and raised it to wrap around his other side, lifting her off the ground. Slowly, he helped her to slide down onto him until he was seated fully within her body. A rush of pleasure and relief burst through her. Finally. It felt like her first time drawing breath in weeks. She'd been desperate for this, her body stretching to accommodate him as he pushed deep inside her.

He cursed before claiming her mouth. His hands gripped her backside and he plunged into her again, wedging her against the wall with his body.

"Yes," she panted, the sound of their bodies coming together as he pumped in and out of her driving her pleasure even higher. "I've felt so empty. My body has been desperate for you, Ash."

It was fast and rough and so intense, and far too quickly, she was nearing her peak. "Harder," she called out as she wrapped her legs more tightly around him. He didn't disappoint as he slammed into her, his ragged breath harsh against her skin as his mouth frantically kissed every part of her he could get to.

Her pleasure peaked so ferociously, it was almost violent. She shouted her pleasure into his mouth and her body contracted around him. A second later, he followed. His roar might have been one of pain. Feeling his seed spill deep inside her only dragged out her own pleasure.

She wasn't sure if it was her body shaking or his. Perhaps both. For several minutes, they simply stayed like that, trying to catch their breath. When their breathing slowed, he lifted her so he could slide out of her body before placing her back on her feet. He supported her with one arm around her waist. The other hand wrapped behind her head and pulled her forehead against his lips. Without a word, he picked her up and carried her to his bed, laying her down gently. Even his bedroom was black like a raven, except for a few hints of deep purple here and there.

"You can't stay all night, but I want to hold you for a few minutes."

She wouldn't argue with that. Wrapped in his arms, she felt fully warm for the first time since leaving Woodburn Hall. Ash pressed his face against her hair and breathed in deeply. "God I've missed this."

She snuggled closer to him, wishing she could feel his skin against hers, but it wasn't to be tonight. "What are we going to do, Ash?"

With a long sigh, he shook his head and pressed a kiss against her temple. "I don't know, Gwen. Give me a few days to figure some things out." He cupped her cheek and turned her face toward him. "Until then, I promise to keep playing the piano for you, but you can't come to my room again. Is that fair?" He pressed his lips to hers, gently this time. "You need to go to bed before you're missed."

When she woke later in the day, Gwen was still in a euphoric state of bliss. She was deliciously tender between her legs from their rough coupling, and she could feel him with every step she took throughout the afternoon.

That night, as she posed with the other girls, moving her body, she wished Ash was on the gaming floor so that she could see him. He spent most of his time up on the balcony watching over everything. Perhaps he was watching her now. She looked up at the hidden place where he usually stood and pressed her chest out a bit more.

An hour later, Ash did appear at the curtain in the back, but he wasn't looking at her. He waved Patrick over and they shared a tense exchange. There was a fire in his eyes, and suddenly she knew. They'd found Greg and he was getting everything secured so that he could leave the Den and go after him. He disappeared back through the curtain, and O'Connell followed him.

She'd be in trouble for leaving her post, but she had to

know what was happening. She had to tell him to be careful. She skirted along the edge of the room and slipped through the heavy curtains. She opened the door to the stairs and hurried up them. O'Connell was just about to lock the door to the hallway that led across to Raven House.

"Wait, I need to go through."

"Very well, but we have to be quick," he said grumpily. She had to jog to keep up with his swift strides as they traversed the long corridor. He unlocked the door at the other end, just long enough for her to get through and then locked it behind her.

There was no sign of Ash and not a sound coming from his private quarters. She hurried down the stairs and around to the backdoor where she finally spotted him giving instructions to the doorman. Fogg was already on a horse and held the reins of a second that was just waiting for Ash to climb into the saddle.

"Gwen?" He hurried over to her. "Is something wrong?"

She swallowed nervously. "You're going after him, aren't you?"

"Yes," he said with a nod. "We are."

She placed a hand over his heart and looked into his eyes. "Remember, he isn't worth your soul."

He gave her a sad smile. "You needn't worry yourself about my soul, Gwen."

"I just—" She paused for a moment, gathering the

courage to say the words that were begging to be spoken. "I just love you."

His eyes grew wide and disbelieving, but then the sadness vanished from his smile.

He lifted her chin in his palm and pressed a lingering kiss to her lips. "I just love you too, Angel."

And then he was gone.

CHAPTER
SIXTEEN

As Ash rode with Fogg beside him, Gwen's sweet words spurred him on. She loved him. And now, he was finally going to meet the monster who'd hurt her. Soon, he would make him pay.

Rage, and a frisson of excitement crackled through his veins. They had him in an abandoned warehouse Ash owned near the docks. He'd known it would come in handy one day for something. Admittedly, this wasn't originally what he'd had in mind.

As they approached the warehouse, a man stepped out of the shadows.

"Alex will take care of the horses and ensure the doors are secure while we're inside," Fogg explained as he climbed down.

Ash gave the man a nod of thanks.

"Before we go in," Fogg said, "I have something for

you that I think you'll like. We found this hanging on the bookshelves in his study, inside that house." He held up a leather strap. Ash ran his hand along its length, a vicious smile growing on his lips. Perhaps tonight's justice would be even more poetic than he had imagined.

"This might be one of the best gifts anyone has ever given me. Hold on to it until I need it."

Inside the large warehouse, several lanterns were lit allowing him to clearly see the scum he'd come for. The man sat on a crate, his hands tied behind his back, two large men flanking him. Ash recognized Brennan, but the other man was unfamiliar. He shot a look at Fogg who gave him a nod of reassurance. This man could be trusted, and understood what he was here for.

"Thank you for bringing him in alive, gentlemen."

"We didn't hurt a hair on his pretty little head," Brennan said. "We left that pleasure for you." The swine was a bit foppish, truth be told. His too long, curly hair hung over his forehead. He wore no coat or waistcoat, so either they'd grabbed him when he wasn't wearing them, or they'd removed them, knowing Ash would want to be rid of them anyway.

"Do you know who I am?" the man said pompously.

Ash stepped forward and allowed his gaze to travel over him, derision, no doubt, plain on his face. "Of course I know who you are, Frederick. Or should I call you Gregory, since that's the name you used on the marriage license? I am glad to finally meet you. You've been a hard man to track down."

"And who are you?" The man sneered. His nasally sniveling voice irritated Ash even more. Ash slowly removed his coat and handed it off to Fogg along with his hat and cane.

When he turned back, he flicked his hand in an upward motion and the two men pulled Frederick to his feet. Ash leaned in close and spoke with a deadly calm. "I'm the man who's come to deliver your punishment." Frederick scowled and Ash slammed a fist into his stomach, knocking the wind from him in a whoosh. He groaned, unable to double over because he was being held upright. He coughed and sputtered as he frantically tried to draw in a breath. Ash basked in the satisfaction brought by the panic on his face.

"So tell me, Greg." He used the name as a taunt. "Why Gwen? Why did you choose her?"

"I don't know what you're talking about."

Ash drove another punch into his stomach. "This will go easier for you if you answer my questions honestly. Now, why did you choose Gwen?"

"Because she looked like my wife." He struggled to get the words out between his labored breaths.

"There, see? That wasn't so hard." Frederick flinched as Ash clapped him on the shoulder.

"So, you thought if you made a baby with a woman

who looked like your wife, you could more easily pass the child off as your own."

He nodded, still panting.

"How did you learn about Warwick?"

He half shrugged. "If you visit the right kind of pub you can find anything you're looking for."

"Even if that thing is a fake marriage to a woman so that you can abuse and rape her to your heart's desire?"

"I did no such thing. She was nothing but a worthless maid and I gave her a better life than she deserved."

Rage erupted inside Ash's chest. With a roar, he threw his fist into the man's stomach three times. He reached a shaking hand behind him and Fogg placed the leather strap inside.

He held it up in front of Frederick as the man panted breathlessly. "Do you recognize this?"

"No," he wheezed.

"Well then, perhaps the sting of it against your skin will jar some memories loose."

"Untie his hands." Of course Frederick tried to run once they were loose, but he didn't stand a chance against those two men.

"I didn't say you could leave, Greg."

"You can't do this!" he shouted, hoarsely.

"I think you'll find I can, Greg."

"That isn't my name! When my father hears about this, you'll be sorry."

"Oh, Greg. Do you really want daddy to know what you've been up to? If I understand correctly, you won't inherit anything if you don't produce a son. I'd hate to think what might happen if he learns you've been committing bigamy in order to try to deceive him. That would bring scandal down on the entire barony if it got out."

"How do you know anything about my inheritance?"

"I have people." He gestured to the other men in the warehouse. "Now, I'm going to be really nice and give you a choice, Greg." He spoke the words as if he were addressing a child. "Option one, you can cooperate and remove your own clothes, which means you'll still have them intact to put back on when we're finished here. Or option two, these men can remove your clothes for you, but I doubt there will be much left of them for you to cover yourself with after they've been ripped from your body."

"You wouldn't dare," he snarled.

"Remove the shirt." The words were quiet and simple. Frederick squealed, and within only a few seconds, his shirt was ripped to shreds on the floor.

His body began to shake violently, his eyes wide with terror. An approving rumble vibrated in Ash's chest. This was the fear he'd been waiting for. The horror he'd dreamt of seeing in this man's eyes for far too long.

"Are you going to kill me?" he asked softly.

"Well, Greg, probably not today. And do you know why?"

"W-why?" he stuttered.

"Because Gwen asked me not to. You see, she seems to think that your life isn't worth blackening my soul for." Ash shrugged. "I tried to tell her that my soul is already damned, but she didn't believe me." The truth was, it never would have occurred to him to *not* kill the man if it weren't for Gwen.

Frederick nodded insistently. "She wouldn't want you to do any of this."

Ash threw back his head and roared with laughter, all of his men laughing with him. "Well, unfortunately for you, Greg, she isn't here. So I'll tell you what I am going to do. I'm going to make sure that your body has more marks on it than all the marks you've ever given her combined." He held up the leather strap. "And the ones I make will be permanent."

He swallowed hard, shaking his head. "Please don't do this."

Ash gripped his chin roughly. "What did you do when she begged you not to beat her? Did you spare her?"

His eyes were wide with panic, but his only answer was a whimper.

"That's what I thought. Now, are you going to remove your trousers, or are they going to go the same way as your shirt?" Ash unbuttoned his own waistcoat as he spoke.

The man began blubbering incoherently.

"Aw, don't start crying already, Greg. We haven't even

gotten to the fun part yet." He loosened his tie and handed it and the waistcoat to Fogg.

"P-p-please don't do this."

Ash gestured with his chin and the men reached for Frederick's trousers. He squealed.

"No! I'll do it! I'll do it!" The words were a high-pitched scream.

Ash held up a hand to stop them. "You'd better make it quick, Greg. Patience is not one of my stronger virtues."

To his credit, he did make fairly quick work of getting them off along with his shoes, and then he stood, bawling, in just his underwear.

Ash raised an impatient brow. "You haven't finished yet, Greg. Do you need more help?"

"No," he cried as he pushed them down. When he was finally naked, he cupped his hands over his manhood. Ash allowed him that for the moment, even though he probably didn't deserve the small amount of dignity.

"Why are you doing this?" His voice was unsteady and jerked with his sobs.

"I think we've already established that, Greg. These are your consequences for what you did to Gwen. For the pain and torment you caused her." He held up the leather strap again. "Do you recognize this yet?"

He nodded shakily. "Yes." The word came out as a desperate whisper. He seemed to hope that if he was honest, he might escape further punishment.

"Good. Then you'll know what comes next."

He started shaking his head frantically. "No, don't do this." He took a step back, but two sets of hands immediately stopped him.

"Are you going to lay yourself over this crate, Greg? Or do they need to help you?" Ash removed his cufflinks and began rolling up his black sleeves.

Sheer panic set in then and Frederick began to scream. "No! Don't do this!" He swung his arms and struggled against his captors, his efforts utterly pointless. He kicked his feet and jerked wildly as they forced his naked body over the crate. Ash delighted in every moment of this man's anguish. This was how he'd earned his reputation in Raven Row, after all. When a person hurt someone he cared about, Ash didn't waver in dispensing swift justice. And since the person this man had hurt was Gwen, administering his punishment would be especially sweet.

He leaned down and spoke softly into Frederick's ear. "Can you imagine how scared she must have been when you forced her to submit to your beatings time and time again? Beatings from a man who'd convinced her he loved her. A man she trusted."

Ash straightened. The leather strap sang as he swung it forcefully through the air. It licked across Frederick's back with a sharp crack and a scream ripped from his throat. He repeated the action several more times, each resulting in a similar scream. Every lash brought Ash a sort of ruthless joy. This man, this monster, had hurt his angel.

He stopped and leaned down to speak into the man's ear, once more. "You see, Greg, Gwen was, and is, under my protection. No one hurts someone I care about without paying for it."

"I'm sorry. Please, no more," he begged.

"Oh, we're just getting started, Greg." Ash stood and flicked the strap across his flesh again. "By the time I'm finished with you, there will be stripes all the way from your shoulders to your knees."

He sobbed and struggled fruitlessly against the men restraining him. Ash continued to swing, stroke after stroke, letting all his rage pour out of him through the strap. As the lashes moved lower on Frederick's back, the two men shifted his body making it easier for him to continue his flogging. He didn't feel an inkling of sympathy as he laid down marks across the man's backside. If anything, he was even more heavy handed on that part of his anatomy because of the memory of the marks he'd seen on Gwen.

True to his word, Ash didn't stop swinging until he reached the bottom of the man's thighs. The entire back side of his body was bloody and raw. Angry welts, many of them oozing blood, streaked over his skin. He wasn't even fighting anymore. Perhaps he'd fainted. Ash looked down at his face. No, he was conscious. His eyes were open, at least, and his chest was still heaving, so he hadn't died.

Ash was also breathing hard from his exertions, his right arm growing weak with exhaustion. He'd savor the soreness from this for days to come.

"I should force myself into your body now, like you used to do to Gwen after you'd finished beating her."

Frederick finally gasped.

"I'm not sure I have the stomach for it, but maybe one of these other gents?"

Brennan stepped up and kicked the man's legs apart. "I'll do it, boss."

"There, you see? Now that's loyalty."

Frederick started screaming again. "No! Please no!"

"Get him up," Ash ordered. He wasn't in the business of rape. Not even with scum like this man.

They hoisted him upright, holding his weight since he didn't seem capable of keeping himself up.

"Here's what's going to happen, Greg. You and your wife are going to leave this country. I don't care if you go to the continent or to America, hell, I don't care if you go to Africa, but you are no longer welcome here."

"I can't. I can't do that. How am I supposed to do that?" The quiet words were meant to be an argument, but there was no fight left in the man.

Ash shrugged. "That's not my problem, Greg. The choice is yours, but I'm going to be keeping a very close eye on you, and if you're still here at the week's end, I will come for you again." He grasped the man's chin, forcing him to meet his eyes. "Next time I won't be nearly so nice. Do I make myself clear?"

He nodded, tears streaming down his pathetic face. "Yes."

"Yes, my lord," Ash corrected.

Frederick's eyes bulged, his brow furrowed with confusion as he slowly repeated the words. "Yes, my lord."

"If I ever hear that you have done anything to harm another woman, that day will be your last. Is that clear?"

"Yes, my lord," he said again, his voice cracking.

With a nod, the two men let him go and he crumpled where he stood. "These men will give you fifteen minutes to get your clothes and get out of my warehouse. If you're not gone by then, they'll drag you out and dump your naked body on the docks."

Ash turned and walked out into the darkness. Except it wasn't complete darkness. He'd been in there longer than he realized. The sky was beginning to lighten and the sun would be dawning within the next hour or so. He closed his eyes and inhaled a long breath, slowly blowing it out. The man had been punished and administering it had been exactly the sweet catharsis his soul had craved.

Fogg stepped out of the warehouse and placed a hand on Ash's shoulder. "Better?"

Ash nodded, and handed over the leather strap, a satisfied smile turning up his lips. "That felt good. I needed that more than you can imagine. Thank you for facilitating all of this."

"Of course, Ash. I may do stupid things occasionally, but my loyalty will always be to you." He began unrolling Ash's sleeves and replaced the cufflinks. He tied his tie and buttoned his waistcoat before holding up Ash's coat.

"I appreciate you, Fogg." Ash slipped his arms into the garment as Alex approached with their horses. "Make sure someone stays on him. I want to know exactly when he leaves the country and where he goes."

Fogg nodded and handed him his hat. "They won't let him out of their sight until I tell them otherwise."

"I need to get back to Gwen. She'll be worried about me, I'm sure." Taking his cane from Fogg, he climbed into the saddle and they started for home.

"Did I hear you tell her you love her?"

"Yes." He let out a sigh. He didn't doubt that it was true, but what was he going to do about it?

"Is she really the reason you didn't kill the bastard?"

Ash nodded. "That's the other thing she said to me before we left."

Fogg chuckled softly. "I never thought I'd see the day that you, Ash, would be brought to heel by a woman."

Ash shrugged. "Neither did I, Fogg. Neither did I."

CHAPTER
SEVENTEEN

As Ash climbed down from his horse, the doorman hurried out to greet him.

"There's a Simon Allister here to see you, boss. He's waiting outside your office."

"At this hour?"

The man shrugged awkwardly.

"Would you like me to let him know you're unavailable right now?" Fogg asked.

Ash shook his head with a sigh. "No. I might as well get this over with. What I need you to do is go inside and find Gwen. I can't have her making a scene right now. If it can be done discreetly, get her up to my chambers so I can talk to her when I'm finished. And I'm sure this goes without saying, but please don't share any details with her."

Fogg nodded, then he licked his thumb and rubbed it on Ash's cheek.

Ash grimaced. "Did you just wipe saliva on me?"

Fogg shrugged. "I couldn't very well send you in there with blood on your face, and I don't happen to have a wash basin out here."

Ash choked on a laugh. "Christ. Well, is there anymore?" He held his face in the light for Fogg's inspection.

"There is, as it happens." He wiped three more spots with his spit covered thumb.

"Jesus. How the mighty have fallen. The Earl of Ashdown out here being washed by his valet's saliva and being demanded an audience with an uninvited guest before dawn has even broken."

Fogg chuckled. "I'm sorry."

"It's not your fault."

"For what it's worth, Ash, he's a good man."

"Perhaps, but he has terrible timing. Go find Gwen. If she's not just inside, check the stairs to my chambers. I'll be up shortly."

Ash gave Fogg a few minutes to deal with Gwen before he went inside. All of the other ladies were in bed, so the house was quiet.

"Mr. Allister." He gave a nod as he approached the man standing beside his office door.

"Lord Ashdown."

Ash shook his head sharply, a scowl settling over his

face. He unlocked the door and waved the man inside before closing them in. He was tired and grumpy, and he didn't want to deal with whatever this was right now.

"I don't use my title here. It's just Ash." He settled himself behind his desk.

Allister nodded. "Apologies."

"Do the intelligence services routinely call upon people before dawn?"

"Not routinely, no. But I had heard that this time of day might be a good time to catch you."

"I have a lot on my plate at the moment, let's just get right to it. Tell me what it is the intelligence services want from me, so I can tell you no, and you can be on your way."

Allister didn't respond immediately. His face was blank and completely unreadable, even for Ash.

"The truth is, it isn't the intelligence services who want your help. It's me."

Ash sighed. He didn't like being misled. "And you thought the best way to go about trying to gain my assistance was to lie to me?"

Ah, there it was. Finally, a tell Ash could read to know what the man was feeling. A deep breath and an involuntary tic beside his eye. He was nervous and wondering now if he'd made an error. He was good at hiding his emotions, but Ash was better at reading them.

"Perhaps it wasn't the best decision, but I didn't know if you'd see me otherwise."

"And what help could I possibly offer you that your employer cannot?"

"My personal problems are not the concern of the intelligence services."

Ash shrugged. "Well, I guess you've given your loyalty to the wrong people then. For the people who work for me, their problems are my problems."

He nodded slowly. "Not all of us are so lucky."

"I have something important to see to, Allister, so what is it you need help with?" Ash was getting impatient.

"I can't afford to pay you, but I was hoping perhaps I could offer you my services in some way in exchange for your assistance with a delicate matter."

"I have no interest in the services of someone who isn't loyal only to me."

Allister closed his eyes briefly. It was obviously something important to him, but Ash didn't have time or patience for games tonight. Gwen was upstairs waiting for him.

"Very well," Allister said after a moment, his jaw clenching tightly. He got to his feet and placed his hat atop his head. "Before I go, you should know, you have blood on your hands."

"What is that supposed to mean?" he said irritably. Was the man accusing him of something?

"It means, you have blood"—he looked down at the desk—"on your hands."

Ash looked down, there were flecks of blood covering the back of his right hand that rested on top of the desk. Christ. He must have it all over him.

He sighed, weariness settling over him. "It's been a long night."

Allister nodded but didn't say anything more.

"When you're ready to offer me your loyalty, Allister, come back and we can talk."

"I don't really have that luxury. There are others I have to consider besides myself." And with that, he left.

Ash shook his head. What a waste of time. He left his office and tracked down some water and a cloth. He cleaned the blood from his hands and wiped his face for good measure. He couldn't very well strip down and wash his whole body, so it would have to do for now.

When Ash entered his chambers a few minutes later, Gwen sat on his piano bench, her arms wrapped tightly around one of his pillows. Tears streamed down her cheeks and her eyes were red and swollen. She dropped the pillow, scrambled off of the bench, and sprinted toward him.

"It's alright, Gwen." He grabbed her shoulders and held her away from him. "I'm sorry love, but I can't hold you yet. I need to get cleaned up first. Can you give me just a few more minutes?" He hated his inability to comfort her immediately.

She nodded and sniffled, her breathing jerky.

"Shhh. Come and wait for me in my bedroom and I'll be right back."

Fogg was in there, his eyes wide with terror. Ash sent him out with a flick of his head. "Make yourself comfortable, Gwen. I'll be back in just a few minutes, and I promise to hold you for as long as you need."

Fogg stood just outside the door. Ash shooed him ahead to the dressing room. "What are you looking so terrified of?"

"There is nothing more frightening than a crying woman."

Ash rolled his eyes. He dealt with crying women on a weekly basis. "Get me something to wash with."

"I already have."

Of course he had. "Then help me get these off. Apparently I'm covered in blood spatter. Allister brought it to my attention on my hands, and since it was on my face too, it must be all over my clothes, as well."

"Thank God they're all black, so I don't have to try to get the stains out." Ever the pragmatist. Once all of Ash's clothes were off, Fogg gave his entire body a quick wipe to get rid of any blood, sweat, or dirt. When he was finished, Ash bent over and dunked his hair in the basin. He didn't want any of this grime anywhere near Gwen.

He rubbed his hair as dry as he could with a towel, along with the rest of him. Fogg gave his hair a quick comb, then held up his robe and he slipped his arms through the sleeves.

"Do you need anything else, Ash?"

"No, in fact, you might go and follow up and make sure everything was taken care of at the warehouse."

He nodded. "I'll be sure to stay away for a few hours."

"Thank you, Fogg. I owe you for all of this."

———

Gwen was curled up under Ash's heavy blankets when he returned to his room, wrapped in a black velvet robe, his feet bare and his hair damp. She climbed out of the bed, desperate to be in his arms. He held her so tight she could barely breathe, and it was heavenly. He rocked her gently, placing kisses on the top of her head. Several minutes passed before he finally spoke.

"What do you want from me right now, Gwen?"

She looked up at him, afraid he would reject what she wanted. "I want to feel your skin against mine."

He untied her sash and helped her to shrug out of her robe before pulling her nightgown over her head. Then he quickly removed his own robe and wrapped his arms back around her. His skin was warm against hers, but it didn't help to thaw the ice that had settled inside her after he'd left.

"Why don't we get under the blankets?" he suggested.

He climbed into the bed and pulled her back tightly against his chest, tucking the blanket snuggly around her.

"What has you so upset, Angel?"

Hearing him call her Angel should have comforted her, but instead, sobs broke over her again. She tried to talk through her crying, as best she could.

"It's silly, really. I should just be happy you're back."

"It's not silly. Tell me everything."

It felt silly to her. She should be pleased. He'd said he loved her. She hadn't expected him to say it back, and hearing it had shocked her. But what if it wasn't real? She'd been fooled before. And even if it was real, what if he still sent her away? Sarah had said she'd have to be sent away.

"I think I'm just a little overwhelmed and more emotional than I should be probably." He didn't say anything, just held her close and waited for her to continue.

"I was worried about you."

"I knew you would be, but you didn't need to be."

"Is he... Is he dead?"

She felt his head shake on top of hers. "No. He's not. But I promise he'll never be a threat to you again."

She turned enough that she could see his face. "Because I asked you not to?"

He pressed a kiss against her temple. "Of course."

He'd spared Greg, and spared his soul, for her. For some reason, it felt like a huge sacrifice. She turned and snuggled back against him. As she wiggled, she felt his manhood begin to come to life against her backside and her stomach fluttered.

He just ignored it. "What else are you upset about? With all those tears, I know there's more than that."

Part of her just wanted to forget it all and ask him to make love to her again instead. Obviously he wanted that. But she also needed answers.

"Sarah reprimanded me, as I deserved, but she knows about us, and I'm afraid she'll make you send me away." She sucked in a deep, shuddering breath as pain gripped her heart.

His soft lips pressed against her neck. "I know it doesn't seem like it sometimes, but I am actually the person in charge here. I'm not going to send you away. I need you here with me." His hand skimmed up her stomach to claim her breast. She moaned and felt him grow even more aroused against her bottom.

"But what does that mean? You need me here with you?" She was growing breathless as searing, open-mouthed kisses moved languidly over her shoulder.

He stopped. "I don't know yet."

"Don't stop, Ash." She felt his lips turn up in a smile against her shoulder. His thumb brushed over her nipple making it pucker and sending a flash of desire straight to her core. She wiggled her bottom against him.

"I'm not going to be able to finish this conversation if you keep that up."

"You started it," she said teasingly.

"So I did." He gently rolled her nipple, coaxing a moan from her. "Perhaps I should make love to you, and then we can finish our conversation."

"What about your rules?"

His lips had moved up her neck and his tongue stopped just behind her ear. "No more rules. Not with you, Angel."

Joy flooded her heart. "Then what are you waiting for?"

With a rumbling groan, he turned her onto her back and his lips descended. Any sadness or fear she'd felt was vanquished by the hunger of his kisses. His firm mouth demanded a response, which she eagerly gave. She opened for him and his tongue swept in to claim every recess of her mouth. Fiery desire rushed through her, finally chasing away the chill that had settled while he was gone.

She gasped with surprised pleasure as his fingers dipped suddenly between her legs. She was already wet and so ready for him and he hummed his appreciation against her mouth. He left her lips and looked into her eyes as he slid a finger inside of her. There was something incredibly intimate about him watching her reaction and it made her excitement soar.

"Yes. Just like that." Her mind emptied of everything else as his thumb swirled against her sensitive nub, sending pleasure spiraling through her body. Her hips lurched, driving his finger even deeper.

"Jesus, Gwen. You make me lose all control. I need to be inside you."

She nodded urgently and spread her legs wide for him. He settled himself between them, his mouth claiming hers for another passionate kiss. He nudged against her entrance. "May I?"

Gwen laughed impatiently. "Are you always going to ask permission?"

His smile was bordering on apologetic as he nodded. "Probably."

How was it possible that a single word could make her love him even more? She lifted her head from the pillow to press a kiss to his lips. "Yes you may, my love."

There was such tenderness in his eyes as he guided himself gently into her body. He rocked slowly in and out of her, his gaze locked on hers as if transfixed. Pleasure whirled through her body as he poured his soul into her.

Her nipples were aching desperately, so without even thinking, she reached between their bodies and grasped them between her fingers. The action, and especially the resulting bolt of pleasure, shocked her and she gasped.

"Christ," he growled, his body jerking with his overwhelming need.

She'd never felt more powerful than she did in that moment. Slowly, she rolled her nipples between fingers and thumbs, making sure he had full view.

Ash was panting as his rhythmic thrusting accelerated. "You, my little minx, are going to send me right over the edge. Give me your fingers." He opened his mouth and she tentatively held out her fingers. He sucked on her thumb and forefinger, wetting them both thoroughly.

"Now do it." He motioned his chin toward her breast.

The wet fingers somehow made the sensations far more powerful. She groaned as pleasure rippled through her body. She held out her other fingers and he smiled before sucking them into his mouth. Rubbing wet fingers over both nipples simultaneously sent her spiraling toward that now familiar peak of ecstasy.

"Ash." His name came out as a desperate plea. She wrapped her legs around him and urged him deeper into her body, needing as much of him as she could get.

Her thighs shook as her pleasure heightened, intense tendrils spreading to her nipples as a burgeoning need for release filled the rest of her body.

He dipped his head down and kissed her briefly. "I want to watch your face as you lose yourself to the pleasure." His voice was deep and it trembled with his own need.

His declaration was the final nudge she needed and a maelstrom of sensation burst through her body. She tried to meet his eyes, but as a surge of pleasure overcame her, her body took command, and she lost all control. She threw back her head, screaming her release.

He roared a curse as his own climax came, his body tensing, sending his seed spilling deep inside her. Sweat glistened over his forehead as he smiled down at her, his breaths coming hard and fast.

"I meant what I said earlier, Angel." His eyes met hers unwaveringly. "I love you."

Tears welled in her eyes. How could she ever have doubted it? "I love you, Ash."

He kissed her forehead tenderly before collapsing onto the bed and pulling her into his embrace, once more.

"Now we just have to figure out what to do with that." He murmured the words softly and pressed a kiss to her hair. "But perhaps we can sleep for a few hours first. It's been such a long night."

"Just as long as you promise you won't leave me to wake up alone."

He gently placed his large hand possessively over her breast and pulled her more tightly against him. "I promise."

EIGHTEEN

A smile grew on Gwen's lips as she came awake. He was still there, surrounding her with his warmth. His arm draped heavily over her body. She could tell by the light coming in around the curtains, that it was no longer morning. Midafternoon, if she had to guess. Ash's breathing was deep and even, so he must still be asleep.

She shifted carefully so that she could turn and see him. He was perfect, even in sleep. His usually immaculate hair stood up in all directions because he'd gone to sleep with it still wet. His face was relaxed and peaceful, none of the typical worry or tension. His brow was smooth, his dark lashes resting serenely against his cheeks. Even the sharp planes of his nose and jaw somehow seemed softer.

She wanted to stay there in bed with him forever, but

if she did, they would more than likely make love again as soon as he woke up. She needed to understand what their future held. She trusted that he truly did love her, but what did that really mean? Being in love didn't suddenly make everything they were doing acceptable. It wouldn't resolve the problems that were undoubtedly starting to germinate among the other ladies as they speculated what was happening between her and Ash. They needed to talk, and that simply wouldn't happen in his bed.

As gently as she could, she moved from under his arm and slid herself out of the bed. Quietly, she donned her nightgown and robe and settled into the chair near the fireplace. There weren't even embers left in the grate and his bedroom was cold now that she wasn't in his embrace, but she didn't want to disturb him, so she just pulled her feet up inside her robe and curled herself up tight.

A noise came from out in the main area. It was probably Fogg. He'd been so obviously uncomfortable when he'd led her up here as she'd cried. She needed to apologize. Quietly, she pulled the door open and peeked out. Fogg turned and his half smile vanished as soon as he laid eyes on her. They instantly grew wide and Gwen almost laughed. How could she possibly be so frightening? She placed a finger over her lips to keep him quiet as she stepped out and closed the door softly behind her.

She watched him swallow and did chuckle then. "I

promise I won't start crying, Fogg," she said quietly. He still looked horribly uncertain. "And I promise I'm nice."

"I'm sure you are, Miss."

He was a large, fit man who Ash clearly trusted. It was humorous that he was made so uneasy by her. "I want to thank you, Fogg."

He shook his head. "It was nothing, Miss."

"Not for me. For Ash. Thank you for keeping him safe and for always taking such good care of him."

"Of course, Miss. That's my job."

"I don't just mean the obvious things, Fogg. You're probably one of the few people who has seen his scars. Not just the ones on his skin, but the ones on his soul, as well. From what I've witnessed, you've been loyal and protective, and as someone who cares for him, I'm grateful he has you."

His demeanor changed, then. His eyes relaxed and the corners of his lips moved up just a bit, as if he'd nearly smiled. "Thank you for saying so, Miss."

Ash's door opened, and he stepped out. He was wearing his robe, once more. His eyes flicked between Gwen and Fogg. "Is something amiss?"

Fogg shook his head. "I'm sorry, Ash. I didn't mean to disturb you."

"You didn't disturb me. What disturbed me was that my bed got cold." A devilish gleam danced in his eyes. Stepping close behind her, he wrapped an arm around her shoulders and pressed a kiss to the top of her head.

"Since you're awake, I'll see to your fire," Fogg said, and hurried into Ash's bedroom.

Ash chuckled. "This is going to take some getting used to for him."

"Does that mean this is going to be a common thing now?"

"Well, that's what we need to discuss." He let out a long sigh over the top of her head.

"That's why I got out of bed. If I had stayed there, we'd probably be doing something else right now, rather than talking."

"You might be right." His lips nibbled on her ear as his hand reached inside her robe to find her breast. Even with the fabric of her nightgown as a barrier, it was beyond enticing.

"You are making this impossible." She pulled his hand out of her robe and turned to face him.

"I'm sorry." He reached for her hand. "I'll behave myself." He pulled her close. "If I ever get too pushy or do anything you don't like or you don't want, you will tell me, right?"

His look was so tender and concerned. It was obviously important to him. She cupped her hand around his cheek. "Of course, my love."

He turned his head, his soft lips pressing against her palm. "Good."

"So are we going to talk, Ash?"

"Perhaps we should put on proper clothes so we can have a proper conversation."

Gwen removed her hands from his and took a step back. A flicker of doubt passed through her. "Why does it seem like you're avoiding this conversation, Ash?"

He lowered his gaze with a sigh. "I suppose I am, a bit." He looked into her eyes. "The truth is, I'm afraid. I don't know what the right answers are here, and that's never been the case for me before. I've always just known what I wanted and did whatever I had to do to make that happen."

"So what's different now?" Uncertainty made her voice more demanding than she'd meant it to be.

One side of his mouth quirked up in a soft smile. "Well, for starters, this isn't just about what I want. These decisions are just as much yours as they are mine." He paused for a moment before continuing. "Here's what I know to be undeniably true. I want you, Gwen. Not just in my bed, and not just for a moment. I want you forever by my side."

Gwen braced her hands against her stomach, over-whelmed by his declaration. How could that possibly be? Those were the kind of words she'd dreamt of hearing from him for such a long time.

"And I also want this." He held his hands out, gesturing to their surroundings. "I want this club. I want this life. I want to stand on that balcony and watch over people as they celebrate and play and gamble. I want my friends and my partners. I want to take in women and make sure they have a chance at a life that doesn't involve selling their bodies or picking someone's pocket." He winked at her and her heart nearly burst with the love she felt for him.

He shrugged, suddenly looking crestfallen as sadness settled over him. "I don't see how I can possibly have both. Not to mention, I have no idea what you want, and so,"—he breathed a deep sigh—"I'm afraid."

"Oh, Ash. How can you be so brilliant and amazing and wonderful and also completely oblivious? I want those very same things you ridiculous man."

"You do?"

She threw her head back in exasperation. "I told you I love this place, and I also told you I love you."

"But what about a family? Children? I don't believe I'm capable of providing you with that even if I did want it. With my history, and the fact that I've never produced any offspring, I'm guessing that won't happen. I don't want to deprive you of that, Gwen."

She stepped forward and took both of his hands in hers. "If I haven't become pregnant in the past year, I think it's likely I'm barren, anyway. So the real question is what about your heir and your responsibilities to the title?"

He shrugged. "I never planned to have children, or even a wife for that matter. I will be taking a more active role in my estate, but I don't think the next earl will come from my loins, and I don't ever want to live there permanently." He sighed. "As for you being barren, that is yet to be proven. Perhaps *you* were not the reason you didn't conceive. He wasn't able to successfully get his wife with child either. In which case, although I think it extremely unlikely, you could actually be pregnant even now, because I haven't been very careful." He ruffled his hands nervously through his hair.

"Would you be upset if I am carrying your child?" She hadn't even considered the possibility before.

He swallowed as he looked at her. "I've never wanted children for fear that I may be to them what my father was to me. Although, I'm starting to believe that may not be true."

"Of course it isn't true. You would be an incredible father, Ash. I saw you with Maggie. You would dote on your own children, and they would love you."

"This is not a place for raising children, Gwen."

"Perhaps not, but it is a place to be proud of. It's a place you could teach your sons to respect women of any status and a place you can teach your daughters that they deserve to be treated with dignity and respect no matter what. To teach your children that you are more than your title and that there is fulfillment in helping those less fortunate."

He looked into her eyes so intently. It was clear he wasn't sure he could believe what she said, but he was trying to. Slowly, he wrapped his arms around her and pressed a long kiss against her forehead.

"Well, I still think it's unlikely children will ever happen. But I imagine we will have plenty of non-traditional nieces and nephews to spoil. Would that be enough for you to feel fulfilled?"

"As long as I have you by my side, I will be happy."

"There's just one last problem then."

"What's that?"

"You said you didn't want to marry again."

She shook her head. Sometimes he could be incredibly obtuse. "That didn't apply to you, Ash."

"Well then." He dropped down on one knee and her heart began to hammer inside her chest. Was this really happening? "Gwen, my wonderful, beautiful, amazing angel, I don't know what the future will hold for us. We may have difficult decisions and problems to solve, we may have a family that doesn't look like what tradition dictates it should and a life that doesn't fit societal expectations. I may be dark and broody and grumpy and even oblivious. I may want you in my bed far too much. I may not be any good at facing my fears. But I will love you and I will move heaven and earth to make sure you are happy and safe. Will you marry me and walk by my side through whatever life brings us?"

"Of course I will, my love."

In one movement, he stood and lifted her into his arms, pressing his lips against hers. He set her back on her feet and looked deep into her eyes. "I love you, my angel."

"Wait. I have one condition. I want a bathtub like the one at Woodburn."

Amusement flickered in his eyes and he kissed her again. "Done." He wrapped his arms around her and breathed in deeply. "You should have asked for more," he whispered. "I would have given you the stars."

"It would seem congratulations are in order." Fogg's voice startled her as he spoke from the doorway. She'd forgotten he was even there, and an embarrassed giggle bubbled out of her.

"Don't worry, Fogg. I'm sure you'll survive having a woman in the house."

Fogg's expression said he wasn't so sure, but then he turned to look at her and there was a kindness in his eyes. "Perhaps this one."

––––––––

Ash stood on his balcony, as always, and waited for the other three to arrive for their meeting. Excitement and trepidation tussled inside his stomach over the prospect of telling his partners of his sudden betrothal. They would be supportive, of course, but shocked, nonetheless.

When they were all settled around their usual table, his tensions eased a bit. He loved these men like brothers. More than he ever had his actual brother, if he was honest. "Before we talk business, I have an announcement to make." He paused briefly. He hadn't planned any kind of speech for this, so he just surged ahead. "Gwen and I are engaged to be married."

Patrick clapped a hand over his mouth to keep from spraying brandy across the table and began to sputter and cough. When he finally got himself under control he turned his gaze on Ash. "Would you stop making these announcements when my mouth is full?"

Michael's mouth was agape, and even Giles looked utterly stunned. Ash chuckled with amusement. It was exactly the response he'd imagined.

"I know it's a surprise that any woman would agree to take on everything that comes with me." He shrugged. "But she has."

"Congratulations, Ash." Michael raised his glass of barley water in a toast. The others followed suit and they all took turns clinking their glasses with his.

"So what does that mean for—" Giles gestured around at the club.

"I know you'll all think it sounds a bit naive, but for now, not much will change. Gwen will move into my private quarters and stop dancing, of course, but otherwise, I expect things will continue relatively normally."

"And what about when you start a family?" Michael's wife was expecting even now, so of course he'd be the one to ask about that.

"Well, based on—" Ash hesitated, unsure how to

phrase it delicately. "I think a family of our own is unlikely. But if that does happen, we'll cross that bridge when we get to it. We're hopeful that you will allow us our role as aunt and uncle to any children any of you may have."

"We would be honored for our children to have Uncle Ash and Aunt Gwen." Patrick gave a salute with his glass.

"And the same goes for us," Michael promised.

Giles held up his hands. "I'm not having any." He shook his head resolutely.

"We'll see, Giles." Ash raised a brow in his direction. "If I can fall, I'm not sure any man is safe from the clutches of love and marriage."

The other two chuckled. Never could Ash have guessed that the three of them would all one day be madly in love with their wives, but somehow, fate had made it happen. Incredibly, fate had also given him a family, the thing he'd never known he needed or even wanted. A family, not of his blood, but that truly loved him. Gwen, these three men, Trent, and Maggie. Not to mention, Fogg, Sarah, all the ladies at Raven House, and Benson. He might just be the luckiest man alive.

CHAPTER
NINETEEN

As Ash returned to his quarters after closing up his club, excitement hummed in his veins. Would Gwen be there waiting for him? His heart begged for her to be. When he opened the door, she was there, sitting at his piano. No tears this time, only a smile to welcome him home. With her here, it felt more like home than it ever had before. She didn't move from the bench as he closed the door.

"Will you play for me?"

"Perhaps," he said as he sauntered toward her. Of course he would, if he could manage to keep his hands off her and on the keys. The piano was his first love, after all. It had helped him to escape the hell he'd grown up in, and he was glad Gwen enjoyed it, as well. "For a kiss."

He was removing his coat as Fogg walked in from the hall.

"I'll just—" He pointed back down the hallway toward his own room.

"You can take my coat first, if you wouldn't mind."

"Of course," he said nervously. He walked over and Ash handed over his coat.

"And you might as well take these too." Ash unbuttoned his waistcoat and removed his tie. It was a bit ridiculous to pretend like they weren't going to be coming off soon anyway.

Fogg nodded and accepted the garments. "I'm sorry, Ash. I'm not entirely sure how all of this is supposed to work." He gestured between the three of them.

Ash placed a hand on the man's shoulder. "It's new for all of us, Fogg. We'll learn together. There are sure to be some awkward moments along the way, but we'll get there."

That seemed to make him feel a little more at ease. "Would you like a glass of brandy before I make myself scarce?"

"That would be wonderful. Thank you."

He placed his cane on top of the piano and sat down on the bench beside Gwen. He leaned in to whisper in her ear. "Perhaps we should wait on the kiss until Fogg is finished." Her answering giggle warmed his soul.

"Somehow, I've never seen the inside of your coats before." She raised a brow. "Purple?"

He shrugged. "My tailor insists that having a bit of color in my life will make me a happier man, so I allow him to line some of my coats in purple. Don't tell anybody else. It might ruin my fearsome reputation." He winked and delighted in her laugh.

Fogg delivered his glass of brandy, placing it on top of the piano. "If you need anything else, you know where to find me."

Ash nodded and Fogg left to return to his room. "Now, where were we?" He wrapped a hand around the back of Gwen's head and pulled her in. Her lips were soft and sweet as he kissed her, and even though he kept it brief, his passions were instantly ignited. If he really was going to play for her, he had to stop before he couldn't, or wouldn't. Slowly, he pulled his lips from hers and turned to face the piano. At least his fingers knew what to do, even if his mind was preoccupied.

As always, he allowed his heart to flow into the magnificent instrument. His melody started gentle and sweet, a nod to his feelings for Gwen. But as his thoughts turned more passionate, so too did the notes. As a crescendo swelled, his hands landing with more fervor, the chords stronger, the notes resonating through the room, the tempo of her breathing surged as well. Her desire was growing, just as his own.

He slowed his pace, calming his zeal. As desperate as he was to make love to her, he'd really enjoy spending some time with her outside the bedroom first. He brought his song full circle, repeating the first few bars, before slowly bringing it to a peaceful end.

Tears shimmered in Gwen's eyes as he looked over at her. "That was beautiful. I love listening to you play."

He leaned against her shoulder and lowered his head to rest on top of hers. "I love that you love it," he said softly.

"When I sat on the stairs, your melodies always told me how you felt. They made me feel like I had a connection with you in some way."

"Well, you'll never have to sit out there to listen again. I'll play for you anytime you want." A part of him delighted in her open admiration of him.

"Is there anything you can teach me to play?" Her eyes were bright and hopeful.

"Of course." He held her hands gently and showed her where to place her fingers. He taught her a series of chords that she could repeat. Her joyous laugh floated around him every time she made a mistake. Watching her determined attempts and her elated smile when she got it right had him thoroughly enraptured.

Once she was confident with it, he began to improvise a melody to go along with her. Her gleefulness was intoxicating and his laugh echoed hers. It was exhilarating and intimate all at once. He never could have imagined it possible to feel so much love for a person. Especially a woman, as strange as that seemed. He'd always kept himself apart from them, in a way, but with Gwen, it had been impossible from the start. He never should have sent her away that first time.

Guilt slithered in, settling in his stomach, tarnishing this beautiful moment. He stopped playing and straddled the bench, pulling her snuggly into his arms. "I'm sorry, Gwen. I never should have sent you away. I sent you right into that monster's arms, and I am so regretful of it."

She allowed him to hold her without pulling away. "Where has this come from, Ash?"

"I was just thinking about how much I love you."

She sat back then, and looked into his eyes. "You can love me without feeling guilty, you know. First of all, you didn't send me away. I took a position, in a good household, mind you. And second, none of this would have ever happened between us if I had stayed here. I always would have been just one of the many ladies you've saved."

He scoffed and lifted her chin gently. "You were never just one of many, Gwen. You were always special, from the moment I grabbed your wrist when you tried to run off with my watch. I had never been tempted by any of the ladies I'd brought here before. It had always been easy to set myself apart, but not with you." He pressed a soft kiss against her lips. "I always wanted you in ways that were inappropriate."

"I didn't help any with that. I wanted you too, and flirted endlessly with you. You were always telling me off for it." She giggled. "But that's why I needed to go. This never would have happened between us under those circumstances. You never would have allowed it, no matter how tempted you were."

He nodded slowly. She was right, of course. Not that it eased his conscience any.

"And if I hadn't ended up with Greg, I would never have found myself in your cabin, just waiting to be rescued by you once again."

"Well, thank God for that, at least." He wrapped his arms tightly around her.

"Will you tell me what happened with him?" she asked quietly.

"He and his wife have apparently gone to the continent."

"As interesting as that is, it wasn't really what I was asking."

He knew what she was asking, of course. She wanted to know what Ash had done to him. "Are you sure you want to know?"

She nodded against his chest. Perhaps it would make it a little easier if he didn't have to look her in the eye, but he would still spare her the gory details if he could. Not that he would change any of it. He would always protect the people he cared about, no matter what he had to do. He harbored no guilt or shame for his actions in that regard.

"You understand that I had to punish him, right? Not only because he hurt you, but to make sure he didn't just run off and do the same thing to another woman."

She sat up and cupped her hand around his cheek. Her fingers were cool and her touch so tender. Her smile not one of pity or disgust, but one of pride. "My wonderful Ash. Saving women who you don't even know from a monster who never should have been your responsibility."

He shook his head with a sigh. "You make me sound like a savior, Gwen. That, I am not. I took far too much pleasure in bringing that man pain to ever actually be that."

"You still haven't told me what you did."

So much for being able to say it without looking into her eyes. There they were, looking straight into his soul, waiting for his confession.

"I flogged him," he said with a shrug. "My men found a leather strap, hanging from a bookshelf, in the study of the house you lived in." Her eyes grew wide and she breathed in a shaky breath. His jaw clenched at the confirmation that it had been used on her. And then she ducked her head.

"So they know? Your men know that I was punished by him?"

She was embarrassed. "Gwen, look at me." She hesitated a moment, but did eventually raise her eyes to his. "This is not your shame to bear."

She gasped and her hand shot to her mouth. "Fogg knows. He knows everything, doesn't he?" Her cheeks flamed red.

Ash took hold of her hands. He wasn't going to lie. She needed to understand that Fogg was someone she could trust. "Yes. He was the one who gave me the strap. Gwen, I know you don't know him very well, but Fogg is a good man. Perhaps not in the traditional sense, but he's loyal to me, and therefore to you. He's a good man to have on your side. You have no reason to be embarrassed or ashamed."

She buried her face in her palms. "But I was such a badly behaved wife that my husband had to punish me. Repeatedly. It's embarrassing that people know that."

"No, that isn't what happened, Gwen," Ash said firmly. He pulled her hands away and waited for her to look up at him. "Setting aside the fact that he never was your husband, you did not do anything to earn the beatings that he inflicted upon you. He abused you. Do you understand?"

Her brow was furrowed. She was struggling to accept what he was saying. It broke his heart that she actually blamed herself for any of it.

"Did I deserve the beatings my father gave me?"

"Of course you didn't!" Ash simply raised a brow and watched as, slowly, understanding and acceptance settled over her features. She nodded and leaned back into his embrace. "How many strokes did you give him?"

He rubbed his hand in slow circles over her back. "I don't know. I lost count," he admitted.

"Good," she said after a moment. "He promised me fifty strokes if I came back, so I hope it was a lot."

"I'm sure it was at least that many." He pressed a kiss against the top of her head.

"Ash?" She dragged her fingers slowly up his thigh and arousal burst into life inside him, once more. "Will you make love to me so we can forget about everything else?" She cupped her hand around the growing bulge in his trousers and his whole body jerked.

"Christ. You do know how to drive me mad with lust for you." He claimed her mouth, his hand desperately seeking out her breast. He would never tire of having its softness in his palm. "Angel, I will make love to you anytime, anywhere, and I don't need a reason. Now get those clothes off and get into bed," he growled. With giggles floating back behind her, she ran on tiptoes into his bedroom, her robe dropping into a heap on the floor along the way.

It was hard to believe this was real. It was a life he never thought he could have. Ash downed the remainder of his brandy and grabbed his cane. He would be more than happy to bring her pleasure and make her forget everything else.

———

Ash sat at the head of a long table that had been set up inside The Raven's Den, his wife at his side. He couldn't stop smiling. Never could he have imagined this day. All of the most important people in his life sat around the table, celebrating his marriage. It wasn't possible for his heart to be any fuller.

Gwen got to her feet, and Ash squeezed her hand on top of the table. "Are you alright, love?" She nodded, and began to speak over the din.

"I know it isn't usual for the bride to give a speech." She shrugged. "But nothing about any of this is usual." Everyone around the table laughed and then quieted down to listen to her.

"I mostly want to acknowledge everyone here and thank you all for coming and for supporting and celebrating our union. I've never had a family before, at least not for a very long time, but you have all welcomed me with open arms."

She was the most beautiful thing Ash had ever seen. Her skin glowed with happiness, her cheeks flushed from a combination of exhilaration and champagne.

"Daisy, you were the first one to welcome me back. You have been so sweet and kind, even when I was difficult to deal with."

Daisy blew her a kiss and dabbed the corners of her eyes.

"And Rosie, you recognized my pain immediately, and without even knowing me, took me under your wing as if you were my sister."

Rosie reached across the table for Gwen's hand.

"And Patrick."

Patrick looked surprised to be called on by name.

"I think you may have kept my crying a secret from" —Gwen leaned her head in Ash's direction—"and for that I'm grateful."

"What's this?" Ash asked over the table. "Keeping secrets from me?"

"I don't know what she's talking about," Patrick said, placing a hand over his chest with feigned exasperation. But then he leaned in and spoke quietly, cupping a hand around his mouth. "It was only fair since you didn't tell him you'd caught me kissing my wife." Everyone around the table laughed.

"Belle, thank you for helping me get the perfect gown, and Michael, thank you for keeping Ash occupied during my fittings so he wouldn't see me in it before the wedding."

"Why do I feel as if my partners have shifted their loyalty to my wife?"

Gwen continued to make her way around the table. "Trent. Thank you for always being kind, even when I didn't really know who I was. Thank you for stepping up, allowing Ash to return to his home here. And thank you for permitting him to act as uncle to your adorable sister. I never thought I'd see the day that a sweet little girl would have him wrapped right around her finger."

Ash shrugged and nodded. Gwen looked down at him

with a disarming smile. She certainly had him wrapped around *her* finger.

"As for Sarah, thank you for putting up with me. I know I caused more than my share of problems in a very short period of time. And the same goes for the rest of you ladies. I hope you'll forgive me, and I love you all."

They all got up from their chairs and hurried around the table to crush her in a giant hug. Ash was nearly brought to tears by the love these people had shown his wife. He really was surrounded by the most incredible people.

"And last, but certainly not least, Fogg. I am aware that you have done far more for me than I will ever know, but in addition to that, thank you for so graciously welcoming me into your home. I know it hasn't been easy."

Fogg actually smiled. That was a rare treat, indeed, but he bestowed it upon his wife and gave her nod of appreciation.

The group of people around the table perfectly summed up the life Ash had built. Earls, sitting down and celebrating with his valet and the women who danced in his club. That was what he'd spent his life working for, and pride blossomed within him to see it.

"And then there's Ash." She turned to him, her eyes filled with so much love. "The most incredible, generous, kind, wonderful man I'll ever meet. Somehow, I was lucky enough to have him rescue me... twice."

Ash got to his feet. "She's got it backwards. In truth, she was the one who rescued me. She saw my blackened heart and my tattered soul,"—he shrugged and let out a long sigh—"and somehow, she decided to love me anyway."

"Well, perhaps we rescued each other, then." She pressed a soft kiss against his lips.

She turned back to the table and raised her glass. "To all of you for becoming the family that I never even dreamt I could have."

A cheer went up around the table as they all raised their glasses.

Patrick raised his glass again. "To the bride and groom! May they share a lifetime of happiness!"

"To the bride and groom!" the rest of them echoed around the table.

As Ash gazed into Gwen's eyes, everything else seemed to fade away. His wife. It was hard to believe this could all be real.

"I love you," she said, tears glistening in her eyes.

"And I love you, Angel."

A
Raven
Revived

Lady Jane Kemp is dead. After fleeing an arranged marriage, Daisy, as she's now known, finds refuge as a dancer at a gaming hell. Her new family actually cares about her, and the owners of The Raven's Den provide her protection. She's safe here—until someone from her past shows up, threatening everything.

After losing the love of his life, Gerard Fitzwilliam is a man without a purpose. His ample fortune can't buy happiness, but he uses it to find joy in fits and starts. When he stumbles across The Raven's Den, he discovers not only a remedy for his restlessness, but a place to invest. What he doesn't expect to find there is Lady Jane, alive and well.

Determined to never lose her again, Fitz pledges his love and commitment. They visit her family to inform them she's still alive, and share their happy news before they hear it from someone else. When Daisy disappears once again, Fitz suspects her father might have done something nefarious, but Lord Litchfield is a powerful man. Even with the help of the formidable owners of The Raven's Den, will Fitz ever be able to get Daisy back?

————

About the Author

Taneasha Francis writes historical romance with handsome, grumpy heroes, and the women who steal their hearts. When she's not writing, you'll find her spoiling her adorable beagle or playing the piano and enjoying a glass of sweet tea to recharge her soul.

taneashafrancis.com

Made in United States
Troutdale, OR
11/14/2024

24420177R00159